THAT BAD CARLOS

HARPER & ROW, Publishers / New York, Evanston, and London

THAT BAD CARLOS

by Mina Lewiton

Pictures by Howard Simon

THAT BAD CARLOS

Text copyright © 1964 by Mina Lewiton
Pictures copyright © 1964 by Howard Simon

Printed in the United States of America. All rights reserved. No part of
this book may be used or reproduced in any manner whatsoever without
written permission except in the case of brief quotations embodied in critical
articles and reviews. For information address Harper & Row, Publishers,
Incorporated, 49 East 33rd Street, New York 16, N. Y.

Library of Congress catalog card number: 64-12972

To Eric and Keith Law

How to say the Puerto Rican names:

ANGEL in Spanish is pronounced Ahn-hel. UNCLE JORGE's name is pronounced Hor-hay. MIRAFLORES is Mee-ra-flor-ess. PAQUITA is Pa-kee-ta. FERNANDO is Fair-non-doe. JUANITA is Hwa-nee-ta. MARTINEZ is Mar-teen-ez. MUÑOZ is Moo-nyose. All the other names are easy to say and are pronounced almost exactly as written if you will remember that the *a* in Spanish words and names is always pronounced like the *a* in *dark*.

1

"There is news! Much news!" Mr. Miraflores waved his hands in the air as he hurried into his house. In one hand he held an envelope, in the other a letter fluttered. Under his arm was a newspaper. Mr. Miraflores' eyes were shining and so was his round forehead. "Look! Listen! We are going to New York!"

"Not I," said Carlos. "I am going to stay here, in Paso Doble."

Mr. Miraflores looked severely at Carlos. "Do you wish to be a good boy, Carlos, or a bad one?"

Carlos shrugged his shoulders.

9

"Do not make trouble, Carlos," said Mr. Miraflores in a low voice.

Mr. Miraflores spread the newspaper on the table.

"What is this, Papa?" Carlos asked, pointing to a corner of the newspaper.

"It is a photograph of a lion," said Mr. Miraflores. "This lion is in a zoo in New York. Do you know what a zoo is?"

"No," said Carlos.

"A zoo is a place where animals may be seen. Wild animals, large and small, from all over the world are kept in a zoo. The newspaper says that this lion, whose picture you see here, has been brought from Africa. He lives in the New York zoo."

Carlos studied the lion of the New York zoo.

"Come and see," Mr. Miraflores called to his smaller children who were playing on the floor. "Come and see, Paquita and Fernando, come! Rosa, come!"

Rosa was Mrs. Miraflores. She was combing her hair and at the same time holding up and looking into a tiny mirror.

The younger children came to look at Mr. Mira-flores' newspaper, too. They stood opposite Carlos who was the oldest. Carlos was ten years old.

Last week Carlos's friend, Angel Perez, had given Carlos a photograph of Museo, the baseball player. In the photograph Museo was smiling and his eyes were narrowed. Ever since he had received the photo, Carlos, too, practiced narrowing his eyes. Carlos, while examining the lion's picture, narrowed his eyes.

Paquita, Carlos's sister, was eight. Most of the time Paquita looked cheerful and smiled widely. She had dark brown curly hair that her mother braided tightly into two short, thick braids and tied with bright ribbons.

Fernando, the smallest, was six. He had recently lost two front teeth.

"Not only is there a lion in the zoo, but there is much else in New York. Do you see these tall build-ings?" asked Mr. Miraflores, pointing again to the newspaper. "Do you see how many people are walk-ing in the streets? Look at how many automobiles there are! These are all to be seen in New York. If all goes well, if the airplane tickets arrive safely here from Uncle Jorge, we shall soon be in New York. And when we arrive in New York," Mr. Miraflores said, spreading his fingers and waving his arms, "everything will be different."

"Everything will be different," repeated Paquita, smiling. Then she asked, "What will be different?"

"You will see. Everything is bigger, bigger even than in the big city of San Juan. And besides all this, we will be doing Uncle Jorge a favor. By taking Uncle Jorge's place in his store, he will be able to return home for a visit at last. It is therefore a visit to New York for us, also. It will be something to remember, I assure you."

"I will stay here," said Carlos. "I will stay with Angel, my friend."

"Do not make trouble, Carlos," said Mr. Miraflores in a low voice.

"You do not wish to ride on a plane, Carlos? If you do not go to New York, how can you ride on a plane?" Mrs. Miraflores asked.

Carlos did not reply. He had for a moment forgotten the plane ride.

"You see, it is clear you wish to go to New York," his father said.

"I want to see the animals of the zoo," said Fernando. Fernando made whistling and lisping sounds when he talked because of the two missing front teeth.

"You will not only see the animals when you are in New York, Fernando, but you will ride in a subway."

"What is a subway?" Carlos asked.

"It is a train that runs beneath the street. I have not seen it either, but I have read of it. Also, this is not all of New York," said Mr. Miraflores, turning another page of the newspaper. "This is only one street that we see here."

Carlos and the others stared at the second page of the newspaper. There was a photograph of a boy on a bicycle on this page.

"The postman, Miguel, has a bicycle like this one, and he is not in New York. He is here in Paso Doble," Carlos said.

14

"I can assure you there are thousands of bicycles in New York. It is possible that when we are in New York we will buy one for you. Not immediately, of course, but later on, before we return home. That is, if you are good and not bad, and if the bicycle is not too expensive."

Mrs. Miraflores looked over Mr. Miraflores' shoulder. "The ladies in these photographs are wearing pretty dresses. The hats, particularly, are impressive."

Mrs. Miraflores turned from the newspaper and looked through the open door. Not another person was in sight. A great clump of bougainvillaeas in bright bloom was all that could be seen, and a stretch of dusty road. "It will be interesting to see so many people in one place as there are in New York," she said.

"Do you see the bicycle?" Carlos asked his mother, pointing to the photograph. "Papa will buy me one like this."

His mother laughed. "There are more important things than a bicycle, which is a very expensive thing. First you will have to have new shoes. It does not matter too much that you walk about barefoot here in Paso Doble, but in New York, do you see any barefoot people?"

Carlos, Paquita, Fernando, and Mr. Miraflores searched the photographs.

"There are absolutely no people with bare feet in these photographs," said Mr. Miraflores.

"So," said Mrs. Miraflores, "it is clear the first thing to buy is shoes for everyone and a dress for Paquita. Perhaps even a hat for me. A hat with roses."

"If I had a bicycle," said Carlos, "I could become the postman of New York."

"It is possible," Mr. Miraflores said, looking at Carlos with pride.

"I do not believe it is possible," said Mrs. Miraflores. "We will not remain in New York so long. Everything is different there in any case, as Papa says. Perhaps the postman does not ride on a bicycle, as Miguel does here. Also, Carlos is ten years old. He will have to wait at least ten more years before he is considered old enough to be a postman."

16

But although his mother and father did not agree about the bicycle, his father had promised it, and "before we return home," as he had said. Papa did not break promises. It was as if Carlos already had a bicycle, he was thinking.

The next day was Wednesday. It was the day Miguel came on his bicycle with the letters.

Carlos ran out to meet him. "Miguel, let me have a short ride on your bicycle? To try it out?"

Miguel lifted his shoulders and let them fall. Then he shook his head. "I would like to let you ride on this bicycle, but I am not permitted to do so. It is an official bicycle. In any case, one of my tires is a little flat. I am going home to fix it, as it happens."

"When you are not looking," said Carlos, "I will borrow your bicycle and have a ride."

"That is a bad thing," said Miguel. "It is like stealing."

Carlos said, "I know it is a bad thing, but I do not mind doing a few bad things."

17

"It is better not to do bad things, Carlos," said Miguel. "It is my advice to you."

Miguel gave a letter to Carlos for his father. Miguel rode quickly away.

Papa opened the letter. It contained the airplane tickets for the journey to New York. A letter from Uncle Jorge was enclosed with the tickets. Papa read it aloud:

> I will be happy to return home at last. It is not that I do not like New York. It is only that I am a little tired. You know I am not as young as I used to be, as they say. I would like to see all the family and especially my grandchildren. It will not take long for you to know all there is to know about my store. Paco, I am grateful that you and Rosa and your dear children are coming. I now enclose the tickets for the plane that will bring you quickly here.

"We will be in New York one week from to-morrow," said Mr. Miraflores, holding up his forefinger, "one week!"

"At last," said Mrs. Miraflores, smiling and patting her hair as if already preparing to leave.

"I will stay here," said Carlos, changing his mind

again and forgetting the plane ride, "with my friend, Angel."

"Do not make trouble, Carlos. Do you wish me to think you are a good boy or a bad one?" asked Mr. Miraflores. "Fernando who is only six years old is better behaved than you."

"I am good," said Fernando. "Carlos is the bad one."

"Be quiet, Fernando," said Mama.

Carlos shrugged his shoulders and smiled and went out to find Angel. When he saw him, he said, "Angel, I am going to New York. My father will buy me a bicycle and I will ride on the streets of New York. Perhaps I will be the postman."

"Like Miguel?"

"Like Miguel."

"I wish I could do that," said Angel. "You are a lucky one."

The next Wednesday, when Miguel left his bicycle to deliver a letter to Mrs. Perez, Carlos lifted himself onto the bicycle seat. He found it easy to balance himself and even to ride a few yards. Then Miguel came out.

"Did you forget that only the postman, that is to say, I, am permitted to ride this official bicycle?"

"For one moment I forgot," said Carlos.

"It is better not to do bad things, Carlos. It is my advice to you." Miguel shook his head and rode away.

2

Carlos looked back at the plane, the giant silver kite that had brought him here. It had been in the sky and he had been inside. He looked upward at the deep blue and thought, "In the morning I was in Paso Doble. It is still the same day, but now I am in New York."

It was warm, but not as warm as this morning had been in Paso Doble.

Here, waiting for them, was Uncle Jorge. Carlos recognized Uncle Jorge from a photograph he had sent to Paso Doble.

"I am happy you are here. I am happy to welcome you all. This is a very happy day," Uncle

21

Jorge said, and wiped away a tear. Uncle Jorge, short, round, and white-haired, had brought candy for all the Miraflores', red-striped candy wrapped in transparent wrappers.

The Miraflores family and Uncle Jorge rode through crowded streets in a fast-moving automobile. The people who were walking about looked as they did in the photographs Papa had shown them in the newspaper in Puerto Rico.

Papa said, "There are more people in one street than in all of Paso Doble."

Mrs. Miraflores said, "I see that everything is different. Everything is bigger, more crowded. Also, although I did not buy a hat with roses, I see that many ladies are without hats. Now I do not mind so much not having a hat."

"Yes, everything is different here," said Uncle Jorge, and smiled and sighed and nodded.

Uncle Jorge's store seemed dark and small after the brightness of out-of-doors. It was, however, full of good food smells.

In the back of the store were two rooms in which

the Miraflores' would live with Uncle Jorge until he went home on the plane. There was one small bedroom in which Uncle Jorge slept, and in the other, somewhat larger room there were a number of beds and a table. Most surprising of all the furnishings was a huge, tall, white, shining box. When its door opened, they all shivered with cold.

"This is a refrigerator," said Uncle Jorge. "It makes ice, as you see, and so preserves the food." Inside the refrigerator were many bottles of soda and several inviting dishes of food.

"A truly wonderful place," said Mama, looking about Uncle Jorge's home. "Truly wonderful and astonishing. I am glad to be here."

"The store is remarkable, too," said Papa to Uncle Jorge. "I cannot wait to begin to help you."

"We will all help," said Mama.

"I knew you would like my store," said Uncle Jorge, "and, in fact, all of New York. The children will like it, too. Do you know why? Because of the school. It is an exceptional school. There are hundreds of children in the school, perhaps thousands.

Tomorrow we will take Carlos and Paquita and Fernando to this school. They will have hundreds of friends."

"We will not want to return home," said Mrs. Miraflores, laughing.

"I would like to return now," said Carlos in order to hear his father say, "Do not make trouble, Carlos."

As Carlos expected, his father said in a low voice, "Do not make trouble, Carlos."

Paquita, hearing Carlos, said, "I, too, would like to return."

Fernando, making whistling and lisping sounds, said, "I do not want to return to Paso Doble. I will stay here without them."

It was a school at least fifty times as large as the one in Paso Doble, which had a school consisting of a single room. The name of Carlos's new teacher was Miss Bandler. Miss Bandler was young. She had straight, short dark hair and she wore eye-glasses. She spoke both Spanish and English to the children. At the end of the first day Carlos already knew the English words *okay, hello, good-by,* and *Miss Bandler.*

Each day Carlos learned a little more English from Miss Bandler. Each day Miss Bandler said to Carlos in English as he was leaving, "Good-by, Carlos. You are doing fine. Be sure to speak English and do the homework." Then she said the same thing in Spanish.

Each day Carlos answered, "Okay, Miss Bandler. Good-by." But when he left the classroom, Carlos and the other children of his class at once began to speak Spanish.

One morning Miss Bandler said to the class, "To-day we will study geography. It is a study of the lands and oceans of the whole world."

Miss Bandler revolved the large globe that stood on its own stand in front of her desk.

"Christopher Columbus discovered the New World," she said. "We live in the United States. The United States is part of the New World." On the globe she showed them the United States. It was green in color.

"Here we are." Miss Bandler ran her forefinger

with its shining pink fingernail down the coastline of the United States and then down the coastline of South America. Then her finger traveled around South America, around Cape Horn, up again along North America's western coastline, and into the Arctic Circle.

"Now you have been all around the New World. Now we shall see where Columbus began his travels." Slowly the globe revolved once more.

Miss Bandler said, "Columbus's three sailing vessels with his men in them sailed across this great, great distance. Columbus was seeking a short passage to the East Indies. Instead he discovered what, Margharita?"

Margharita said promptly, "The United States."

"Yes," said Miss Bandler, "he discovered the New World in 1492."

Margharita raised her hand and waved it anxiously. She shouted, "On Columbus Day."

Miss Bandler smiled. "We now call that day Columbus Day. Then it was only known as October twelfth. Very good, Margharita."

The boy who sat beside him said quietly to Carlos in Spanish, "I will be like Columbus. I will look for the New World."

Carlos shook his head and said quietly, too, "It is already discovered as you have heard. Everything is already discovered. Columbus discovered everything. He was the first. You cannot discover it again. But you can go to the moon. In Ricardo's Television and Radio Repair store, around the corner from my uncle's store, there is a television set on which I have seen pictures of the moon."

"I do not wish to go to the moon," said the boy. "I prefer the sea. When I was still small, my father took me with him when we went fishing. That was in Puerto Rico. I would like to go a long distance in a big ship. If I do not discover a new world, I will see at least what is already discovered."

"Not I. I will be a bad guy. I will join a gang," said Carlos, smiling. "Yesterday I saw this on television in Ricardo's Television and Radio Repair store. It is possible I will rob banks."

"You will be caught and you will go to prison," said his neighbor.

"No, I will escape."

"It is often impossible to escape."

"I think for me it will be easy. What is your name?" Carlos asked.

"My name is Angel. Angel Muñoz. And yours?" the boy asked, and looked curiously at Carlos.

"My name is Carlos Miraflores. You remind me of my friend in Puerto Rico," said Carlos. "His name, too, is Angel."

Miss Bandler said, "Please do not whisper in the back of the classroom. If you have something interesting to say, we all wish to hear it. Do you wish to tell us what you were whispering?"

Carlos did not answer, neither did Angel.

Miss Bandler wrote in a little black book.

The gong sounded loudly, and the children all began talking at once, quickly and in Spanish.

"Class dismissed for lunch," said Miss Bandler. "In the afternoon there will be drawing. Carlos Miraflores, please come here."

Carlos came slowly toward Miss Bandler.

3

Miss Bandler was going to ask him what he had been whispering to Angel and he would have to say he had told Angel he was going to be a bad guy. He walked even more slowly toward Miss Bandler.

It seemed Miss Bandler did not wish to speak about the whispering. Miss Bandler said in English, then translated into Spanish, "Here is a quarter and a nickel, Carlos. We will need some fruit for the drawing lesson this afternoon. Your father has a store, is it not so?"

"Yes, it is so, Miss Bandler."

"Is there some fruit for sale in your father's

29

store? We would like to have two oranges and a banana for the drawing lesson."

"We do not have oranges or bananas in our store, but I can easily buy these fruits at the fruit store. There is one that I pass on the way to my house."

"I would like that very much," said Miss Bandler, giving the quarter and the nickel to Carlos.

"Okay," said Carlos. "Good-by, Miss Bandler."

Carlos went hurrying downstairs. On the street Angel was waiting.

"Was Miss Bandler angry because you were talking to me?" asked Angel.

"No, she was not angry."

"I think she was angry. Otherwise why did she talk to you?"

Carlos said, "She asked me to buy some fruit for the drawing lesson this afternoon."

"What will you buy?"

"Oranges and a banana."

"I think it is because you were talking to me that you must now buy this fruit."

"No. There was nothing about talking to you in our conversation."

"Miss Bandler has sharp ears. I think she heard you are going to belong to a gang. Perhaps she will think I, too, wish to belong to a gang."

"Do not be afraid. We did not speak of you."

Angel continued to look serious. "As for me, I am not interested in gangs. I am going to be a pilot of a ship or of an airplane."

"Good-by," said Carlos. "I will see you in the afternoon."

As Carlos turned the corner on his way home there was his mother walking toward him with Paquita and Fernando, who went to school only in the afternoons.

Fernando shouted, "Here comes that bad Carlos."

"Be quiet, Fernando," said his mother, smiling. "You will find your lunch in the house, Carlos. Your father and Uncle Jorge are waiting for you."

During their lunch the bell of the store rang now and then. Carlos went into the store from the back room and sold a box of scouring powder, a bag of potatoes, and two cans of garbanzo beans. Carlos took the money and Uncle Jorge gave him the change to return to the customers.

"Carlos is already a good business man," said Uncle Jorge.

On the way back to school Carlos stopped in front of Frank's California Fruit Market on Broadway. On the fruit stand that was built on the sidewalk in front of the store, the oranges were displayed. A wall was built of oranges as a wall is built of bricks, each orange fitting beside another. Carlos noticed that the largest oranges were in the very bottom row. If he could buy these large oranges and bring them to Miss Bandler, she would see he had carefully selected them. If he could remove one, then the one above would slip down one place, then the one above that, and so on. He would ask Frank to remove two large oranges from the bottom row. He waited, but Frank was busy inside.

Carlos continued to wait. Frank was still weighing vegetables on a scale inside the store. Carlos looked at the bottom row of oranges once more. It would be very easy to get the oranges and not bother Frank to get them. It was getting late. The bananas were nearby. After he had the oranges, he would choose a banana and pay for it and the two oranges. Then he would run to school.

Carlos put out his hand to see if the oranges were stuck tight. No, they were not. It seemed easy to remove one. He firmly took hold of one large orange in the bottom row, but no sooner had he removed it only a little when, suddenly, there was a shower of oranges.

They rained down on him and upon the sidewalk. He could not stop the rolling oranges even with his hands and feet. He ran after them, but they rolled off in all directions. Then he saw Frank.

Frank's face was red and angry. Frank shouted, "Hey, you! If I catch you, you'll be sorry. You better start running!" Frank shook his fist at Carlos, and Carlos took Frank's advice. He ran down one block and up another. He looked back. Frank was not chasing him, but Carlos continued to run.

At the crossing a policeman stood directing traffic.

He looked at Carlos and Carlos stopped running and began to walk quickly, but the policeman continued to stare watchfully at Carlos. Carlos walked another block. He almost forgot he had promised to buy oranges and a banana for Miss Bandler. He would have to buy the fruit for Miss Bandler, although he would surely be late.

He hurried back to Broadway. There he saw another fruit stand. Here the oranges were built up into a pyramid, but Carlos stood waiting, this time, until the owner of the store came outside.

"Eighteen cents for two oranges, five cents for the banana."

Carlos got two cents in change from the quarter and still had the nickel.

"You want another orange?" the man asked, seeing Carlos looking at his coins. "Okay, one more for seven cents." The man took the coins out of Carlos's hand.

Carlos ran to school. He was in the classroom as the gong sounded.

"Thank you, Carlos," said Miss Bandler when he handed her the extra orange, "but we need only two. Take the third orange as a present for yourself."

"Thank you, Miss Bandler."

After school Angel walked home with Carlos and saw the orange in Carlos's hand.

"I observed a strange sight," said Angel, "when I was returning to school this afternoon. All the oranges of Frank's stand were rolling over the street. I think someone upset the oranges. Perhaps is was a leader of a gang that overturns orange stands who did this. Some bad guy, I think, was playing a trick on Frank."

Carlos said nothing.

4

The Miraflores family had been in New York for three weeks.

Just as Uncle Jorge had said, it did not take long for Mama and Papa and even the children to learn to sell the groceries at the marked prices. Everyone who came to the store spoke only Spanish, so that the Miraflores' were almost as much at home in New York as they had been in Puerto Rico.

"New York is a wonderful city," said Mrs. Miraflores, smiling and patting her dark, shining hair. "It is lively. Today there were twenty customers in the store, not counting the children. With children there were perhaps fifty."

37

She said this to Carlos while she was putting yams into a red-and-yellow basket and setting the basket in the store window. At each side of the store window Mrs. Miraflores had arranged streamers of green crepe paper into drawn-back curtains. In the very center of the window she had placed a basket of bright green, not-yet-ripe avocados. The basket of avocados was placed upon rows of garbanzo beans in cans. It was cheerful-looking.

Uncle Jorge said, "Everything is better now. This store has needed a woman's decorative touch. Up to today, ever since I lost poor Juanita, the store has not looked so inviting."

Mr. Miraflores directed the arrangements from outside. When the yams were set beside the avocados, he nodded vigorously. "Beautiful!" he shouted to Mrs. Miraflores. "Very beautiful!"

Mrs. Miraflores came out, too, to admire the store window.

"Do not forget about Mrs. Martinez' order," said Mrs. Miraflores as they went inside. "We promised

38

to send Carlos, as soon as he came from school, with the rest of her groceries."

"I do not forget," said Mr. Miraflores. "I have been waiting for Carlos."

"Where can he be?" asked Mrs. Miraflores, opening the door once more and looking up and down the street. Then she saw him. "He is there!" Mrs. Miraflores said, pointing.

Fernando ran to the door. "There is that bad Carlos. Carlos is trying to fly," said Fernando, looking down the street.

Carlos was standing on the fire hydrant at the corner of the street. By spreading his arms straight out, he kept himself from falling off the hydrant. Now he raised one foot, carefully and slowly, and continued to balance himself although a trifle unsteadily. Without moving his head, he glanced down at his friend, Angel, who was standing nearby.

"You are a true acrobat," said Angel.

Carlos was pleased to hear his friend's opinion. He put both feet on the fire hydrant, firmly, and

slowly bent down, holding on to the knob of the hydrant with both hands. Then gradually he raised his feet in the air while standing on his hands on the fire hydrant. He straightened his feet slowly in the air.

It was at that moment that Carlos heard his father's voice.

"Carlos, come to me," Mr. Miraflores called. "I see books on the sidewalk. Is the sidewalk a place for school books? Pick them up at once. Come to the store."

Carlos waved his feet in the air and turned himself right side up, so that he was standing on his feet and not on his hands. He picked up his books and hurried toward the store. Angel, his friend, went along, but he did not go inside. Angel waited outside.

"Are there no better things to do than to stand on your head?" asked Mr. Miraflores, and did not wait for a reply. "Be good enough to take this carton of groceries to Mrs. Martinez. There is going to be a celebration there this evening. Do you know where Mrs. Martinez, lives?"

"I think I know," said Carlos. "On the corner of Columbus Avenue, on the fifth floor, at the end of this block?"

"No. It is another Mrs. Martinez. This is the one who lives on Sixty-ninth Street in the house with the bar downstairs. On the second floor."

"Okay," said Carlos.

"She is waiting for these groceries. Especially the rice and the tomatoes and the cake. The cake is the most important, as there is to be the celebration I have spoken about."

"Okay," said Carlos again, and picked up the large carton.

When he had gone a little way, Angel joined him. Angel looked at the carton and said, "Wait one moment. I will bring my sister's baby carriage. It will be easier to carry a carton that is so heavy in the baby carriage."

"Okay," said Carlos, "but I will go with you to

get the baby carriage. If I wait here for you, my father may see me. He will tell me to hurry to Mrs. Martinez' without the carriage."

Angel lived a block and a half away.

Carlos reconsidered. "Look, I think it will be quicker if we take this carton of groceries to Sixty-ninth Street. Your house is almost two blocks away, then we must go to Sixty-ninth Street which is another two blocks away."

"When we have the carriage it will take only one moment. A carriage has wheels, so we will be able to run with it. This carton is a heavy one."

"That is true," said Carlos. His hands and arms were already tired.

They held the carton between them and went to Angel's house, but when they got there, Angel could not find his little sister's carriage behind the stairs.

"It may be that my mother has already taken my sister to the park in the carriage. Fortunately here is an old broken carriage. It looks as if it is aban-

43

doned. I do not think it belongs to anyone. We can borrow it. For carrying groceries it is good enough." Angel wheeled it back and forth. One of its wheels was bent deeply inward. "It is better than nothing," said Angel.

5

Carlos and Angel put Mrs. Martinez'
carton of groceries into the baby carriage with the
bent-in wheel and hurried out of the hallway. Together they carefully steered it down the few steps
and into the street.

The bent-in wheel looked as if it might come off
at any moment. As they hurried around the corner
of Sixty-eighth Street it did roll off. Relieved of its
difficult duty, it escaped quickly. Angel ran after
it and brought it back and put it inside the carriage.

"This baby carriage can still roll on three wheels
if we are careful," said Angel. "Later we will put
back the wheel. When we fix this carriage, it will be
better than when we borrowed it."

"Yes, later we will fix it," said Carlos. "Meanwhile we must hurry."

"Perhaps it is better to fix it now," said Angel. "Then we can go more quickly. It is the work of one moment. Let us see if we can find something that will keep this wheel on."

"It will take too long," said Carlos. "I have made a promise. Let us hurry." They put the wheel into the carriage again.

"Angel, Carlos!" someone called to them from half a block away.

It was Felipe Solero, who was also in Miss Bandler's class. Felipe was holding a hard rubber ball in his hands.

"Look, Angel! Look, Carlos!" Felipe shouted to them and threw the ball high out of sight. Then Felipe ran a few steps and caught the ball in one hand as it came down.

"You are a good ballplayer, Felipe," said Angel.

"I will catch the highest ball you wish to throw."

"I would like to throw you a high one," said Angel.

46

"If you wish to play, I will let you both catch this ball. First you, Angel, then you, Carlos."

"We are going somewhere," said Carlos. "Wait for us. When we return, we will play with you, Felipe."

"I am unable to wait until you return. Now I am ready to play. Later, no."

"Okay. One throw and one catch for each one."

Angel and Carlos put the carriage against the red brick wall of a warehouse.

Felipe ran into the street and threw his ball to Angel. Angel missed, but Carlos ran and caught it. Carlos threw it back with all his strength. He saw it curve high in the air. Felipe had to run fast to catch it.

"Now, let us go," said Carlos. "We must deliver the groceries."

"One more minute does not matter," said Angel. "I did not yet catch the ball."

Angel did catch the next ball, but it was an easy one.

"Throw me a high one," shouted Angel, laughing. But when Felipe threw a high one, Angel missed it. The ball went rolling down the street.

"We must go, Felipe," said Carlos, "but we will come back."

Felipe shouted, "You must go? When the ball is lost, you must go. When I had the ball you played with me. It is only right that you should help me look for it now that it is lost."

"Let us help this Felipe find his ball, but then we must bring the groceries to Mrs. Martinez, Angel," said Carlos, hurrying to the carriage with the carton in it. "I will stay here while you help him. "If you do not find it, you will stay here and I will go."

"We will soon find it. Leave the carriage for one moment and together we will find it quickly."

"It is a good new ball," said Felipe, almost in tears. "It is a ball costing seventy-nine cents."

"Someone will find it in a moment. You do not have to cry like a baby," said Angel.

Nevertheless they hurried after Felipe who was looking at the sidewalk and the street. They looked along the curb and down gratings. They asked children along the way if they had seen a red, hard rubber ball. No one had.

They were almost at Central Park when they saw a large black poodle on a leash. A lady in green stretch pants was holding the leash. The dog was carrying a red rubber ball in his mouth.

"There is my ball!" shouted Felipe. "That dog has found my ball. Hey, dog, come on, give me my ball!"

"Say 'please,'" said the lady in green stretch pants.

"Hey, please," said Felipe, crouching down on hands and knees. The dog and the lady stood still and the dog growled. The lady laughed and said, "Say it again and call him by his name. His name is Ruffles. Say 'Please, Ruffles.'"

"Hey, Ruffles, give me my ball, please."

"Please, Ruffles, give Felipe his ball," Angel said softly.

The dog growled at Angel, too.

Angel said, "Give me the ball, Ruffles, and I will give you this dog biscuit. It is the dog biscuit I

save for Rodrigo who lives next door to me."

As soon as the dog saw the biscuit he dropped the ball and snapped up the biscuit that Angel held out to him.

"Drop it, Ruffles," said the lady, but it was too late. Ruffles had already eaten Angel's dog biscuit.

"What kind of dog biscuit was that?" the lady asked Angel crossly.

Angel shrugged. "A dog biscuit from a dog biscuit box. This was a good biscuit."

"I don't allow my dog to eat biscuits that strangers give him," said the lady.

Carlos took Angel by the arm and began to walk rapidly.

"Come back," shouted the lady to Angel who was hurrying away with Carlos. "What was the name on the dog biscuit box?"

Angel turned around and shook his head and shrugged his shoulders.

Carlos and Angel hurried back to the street on which they had left their carriage. When they came

51

to the red brick wall of the warehouse, they saw that the baby carriage was no longer there.

"Someone has stolen our carriage!" said Angel.

"And the groceries for Mrs. Martinez," said Carlos. "Mrs. Martinez will be angry. My father will be even more angry."

"We must find the stolen carriage," said Angel.

"The stolen carriage and the groceries," said Carlos.

"When we find the carriage we will find the groceries," Angel said as if he were a detective.

"I will have to hurry to tell my father," said Carlos, but he did not make a move.

"Wait. Let us first look around. There will be time enough to tell him if we do not succeed. I will ask my sister to help us. When something is lost in our house, Estrellita is the one who finds it."

"This is not something lost in your house, but I will go with you, Angel."

The more Carlos thought about the lost groceries, the less he wanted to tell his father about what had happened. Nor did he want to go to Mrs. Martinez to explain why the groceries were not yet delivered.

Angel said, "The ball was lost. We looked for it and we found it."

But the thought of the ball made Carlos even more unhappy.

6

They began to hurry to Angel's house. On the way they looked from one side of the street to the other, but all the baby carriages had four good wheels and, besides, all the baby carriages had babies sitting or sleeping in them.

As they came around the corner they saw a small crowd on the steps of Angel's house. A few people had gathered on the sidewalk in front of the house, too. Through the crowd on the steps a man with a large black mustache made his way down with a hammer in his hand.

"It is Mr. Fernandez," said Angel. "This is a man who is always angry. He lives on the top floor, but I can hear his voice when I am standing on the sidewalk."

As they came a little closer Angel and Carlos heard Mr. Fernandez say angrily, "Please stand back. Felicia, give me the wheel. I will fix it."

The crowd moved aside for Mr. Fernandez and there, on the sidewalk, at the foot of the stone steps, stood Angel's and Carlos's baby carriage, its three wheels up in the air.

Mrs. Fernandez was handing the needed wheel to her husband.

"Permit him to work, please," said Mrs. Fernandez to the crowd. "Do not stand in his way, at least."

The crowd moved a little but not much. It was as if they had all gathered around Mrs. Fernandez to listen to a speech. Mrs. Fernandez did not disappoint them.

"I will tell you how this has come about," Mrs. Fernandez said. "Only a little while ago, perhaps one hour ago, no, it was a little more than an hour ago, for now it is half-past four and it happened

when I heard the church bells strike three—it was exactly three or possibly a few moments later—and already the carriage was gone."

"What happened?" asked someone. "I have not yet heard what happened."

"Be patient, Mrs. Alegrante," said Mrs. Fernandez, "you will hear the whole story if you will be patient. Each day at three o'clock or perhaps a few moments later, but not too much later, I take Rosita in my arms to bring her to the park in her baby carriage. Today, in the place where Rosita's baby carriage stands what do I find? No carriage. Nothing! The baby carriage is gone. Stolen! Rosita begins to cry. She wants to go to sleep in her carriage as always. I say to her, 'Go to sleep in my arms, Rosita, and I will go and look for your carriage.' At that moment my husband comes downstairs. He, too, begins to look for the carriage. Together we walk down one street, then down another, and meanwhile Rosita falls asleep and is quiet. Then, what do we both see at the same moment? Our carriage! But what has happened to it? It has a missing

wheel. The wheel is no longer attached to the carriage. The carriage is in the condition that you now
see. And where is the wheel? *Inside* the carriage."

"It is not unusual for thieves to take baby carriages," a man remarked.

"On the contrary, I think it is unusual," Mrs.
Fernandez insisted. "And there is one more thing
I must tell you. The thief has been good enough to
leave me a few groceries inside the carriage. So I
say to Ramón, 'It is the least one can expect for the
use of this carriage for the afternoon.' Yet I do not
think it was necessary to break off a wheel. A baby
carriage with four wheels should not be returned
with three. Is it not true?" Mrs. Fernandez de-
manded.

A lady in the crowd replied, "That is perfectly
true."

Another voice inquired, "What groceries did you
find in your carriage, Mrs. Fernandez?"

"Only a few small necessities. A little rice and
a little tomato paste and a cake. A very useful cake.
I bake my own cake when I wish to have a good

one, but this one happens to be the type of cake I like and Ramón likes, also. Entirely of chocolate. There were also some cans of garbanzo beans and a bottle of green olives."

"In my opinion it is a very nice present." The lady who said this laughed loudly.

"But do you see what has happened to the baby carriage?" asked Mrs. Fernandez.

"Excuse me, but it seems to me one of the wheels looked shaky yesterday," said the lady who had laughed.

Mrs. Fernandez did not reply to this.

Mr. Fernandez said angrily, "This baby carriage has been badly treated."

Angel took Carlos by the arm and walked a few steps with him. "Come with me, Carlos. We can find Estrellita inside, I think."

They went upstairs. A few of the doors on each floor stood open.

From one of these someone called out, "Hey, Angel!"

"Estrellita, you are the one we are looking for!"

"I am playing with Rosita, the Fernandez baby. Mrs. Fernandez' carriage was stolen so she could not go to the park and now—"

"The carriage is now found," said Angel.

"I know," said Estrellita, "and do you know that inside the carriage was a carton? Was that not a lucky thing for Mrs. Fernandez? Look, there it is. Instead of losing something, something is found."

"It is very lucky," said Angel.

The carton stood on the table, the groceries not yet removed from it.

Angel said, "Estrellita, they are fixing the carriage. Now that it is almost ready for use, take Rosita downstairs. Soon you can go to the park with this baby and her parents."

"Yes, you are right. I will go with Mrs. Fernandez to the park. I will help her take care of Rosita. I will put on Rosita's new shoes for her."

It seemed to take hours to put on the baby's shoes, but at last they were on Rosita's feet. Estrellita walked to the door with Rosita who was just beginning to learn to walk. She fell down at every other step.

"If you wish," said Angel, beginning to be impatient, "I will carry the baby downstairs. That will be faster."

"She can almost walk as you see," said Estrellita, "but perhaps it is better for her to be carried. The stairs are dangerous for Rosita. I will carry her myself." She picked up Rosita gently and went cautiously down the stairs with her.

When Estrellita had gone down a flight of stairs, Angel whispered, "Carlos, take off your jacket. Put these groceries into your jacket. We will have to take them back with us without the carton. Someone may recognize the carton."

"I do not want to take these groceries away. I think I will go now to Mr. Fernandez and I will explain what has happened. That is the best way."

Angel shook his head. "This Mr. Fernandez has a loud voice as I have told you. And a bad temper. It will be difficult to make explanations to him."

"If we steal these groceries, these people will be even more angry, and they will have a reason for being angry—"

"How can you steal what is yours?" Angel took

off his own jacket. "I will put everything into the jacket. We will run to Mrs. Martinez. There is still time before Mr. Fernandez returns. I do not think the wheel can be easily fixed."

As he spoke, Angel put the box of rice, the cans of tomato paste, the olive bottle, the cans of garbanzo beans and, last of all, and on the top, the chocolate cake, into the jacket that he had laid on the floor. Now he tied the sleeves together to make a sack.

"Carlos," he said, "I do not want you to be in trouble and you do not want to make your father angry. We are going to Mrs. Martinez with her groceries."

7

As quietly as possible Carlos and Angel walked down the stairs, the tied-up jacket between them. They peered out of the doorway.

The crowd was still standing there, at the bottom of the steps and on the sidewalk.

Mr. Fernandez shouted, "Ricardo, I thank you for this hammer, but a heavier one is needed. Could you not borrow a heavier one?"

A tall boy with shining dark hair said, "It is not easy to borrow all sizes of hammers. Let me return this one first and I shall see."

"No," Mr. Fernandez called out, "there is no time to return this one and to choose another. I

63

will do what I can with the disadvantage of a light hammer."

Mr. Fernandez seemed to be having difficulty replacing the wheel, as Angel had said. He had turned the baby carriage upside down and was using the hammer to straighten this or that.

The crowd seemed even larger now and a great many children surrounded Mr. Fernandez. Some old people had joined the crowd, too, and some of these were advising Mr. Fernandez.

"Perhaps a little oil is needed, Mr. Fernandez," said one old lady. "I remember this wheel made a screeching sound. It might as well be oiled now before you put it back."

"We will walk quickly," Angel whispered to Carlos. They moved outside the circle of the crowd that was watching Mr. Fernandez as he tried to replace the wheel.

When they had walked a half block Carlos said, "We cannot bring Mrs. Martinez her groceries in your jacket, Angel. It would be better if we could get a carton. Perhaps you will go to my father and without explanation, simply ask for a carton."

"No. It will arouse suspicion. I do not think your father likes me. Let us not add to our troubles. I will go to the A & P and ask there for a carton. They are always ready to give away cartons. They will not ask questions."

They came to the A & P and Angel went inside and came out promptly. He had acquired a large, new-looking carton.

On the sidewalk, a little to the side of the A & P, Carlos untied the sleeves of the jacket. He transferred Mrs. Martinez' groceries from the jacket into the carton. The cake in its box was a little flatter than originally, but it was not otherwise damaged. They lifted the carton and carried it between them, Carlos and Angel using both their hands.

"We are very fortunate," said Angel, "that everything came out well."

It was then that they saw the policeman.

He looked as if he had been there for a long time, observing them closely.

Perhaps he had been there ever since Carlos had untied the sleeves of the jacket to remove Mrs. Martinez' groceries.

Carlos pretended he did not see the policeman. He looked at the neatly arranged groceries in the carton, then at Angel.

"You see, Angel," Carlos said, "one would not know that this is not the original carton."

The policeman walked slowly toward them and stopped in front of them, as if to prevent them from going on.

"What's this?" he said, frowning, as if everything

were not plainly visible in the carton. Then he asked the same question in Spanish.

Carlos shrugged his shoulders as if to say he himself did not know what it was.

Angel smiled at the policeman. He said in English, "These are groceries for Mrs. Martinez. He"— Angel pointed to Carlos—"my friend, must deliver these groceries to Mrs. Martinez who is having a celebration. It is already late. One hour ago, perhaps two hours ago, this was to be delivered." Angel began to walk and Carlos walked, too, around the policeman, but now the policeman turned and walked beside them.

Then, after a few steps, the policeman stood still. "Where'd you get this stuff?"

Carlos said seriously, "We got it from Mrs. Fernandez." He turned his head in the direction of Angel's house.

"No, not from Mrs. Fernandez," Angel explained patiently, "from your father's store, Carlos."

A few people came to listen to the boys' and the policeman's conversation.

The policeman took out a small notebook. "What's your name?" he asked Carlos.

"Carlos Miraflores."

"Spell it."

Carlos spelled it.

"And you?"

"Angel Muñoz."

He did not ask Angel to spell his name, but he said, "Did you get these things from a store? Didn't one of you just come out of the A & P?"

"Yes," said Carlos, "but the things are from my father's store. Only the carton is not from my father's store. But it is not exactly my father's store. It is Uncle Jorge's store."

"Let's go to the store you got this stuff from," said the policeman.

"We cannot go to my father," said Carlos, not moving.

"Okay," said the policeman. "If we don't go to the store, we go to the station. Let's move."

"I have to bring these things to Mrs. Martinez. I am late already."

68

"Do we go to your father's store?"

Carlos said to the policeman, "He will be angry because these are not already delivered. Also he will not understand why you have come with us."

"We go to the station and we send for your father. Now, on the double!"

More people came to listen to the policeman and Carlos and Angel.

Angel said, "I think we must go to your father's store, Carlos. It is better to go to your father than to ask your father to go to the police station to find you and the groceries of Mrs. Martinez."

"My father will be angry," said Carlos. "And Mrs. Martinez will be angry also."

"Go on home," shouted the policeman to the crowd that now followed them as they began to walk.

The crowd hung back but continued to follow the policeman and the boys who were carrying the groceries.

The boys with their carton and the policeman turned the corner. As they approached Uncle

Jorge's store, Angel saw that another crowd was gathered there. He recognized his father's customer, Mrs. Martinez, who was talking to his father. Not only was Mrs. Martinez there, but, surprisingly, Mr. and Mrs. Fernandez were there, too, and a large crowd of children.

As the policeman and Carlos and Angel came toward the store, Mr. Fernandez saw them and came rushing toward them. He reached for Angel's arm, but Angel did not allow himself to be caught. He wriggled away and stood at a little distance, prepared to run if necessary.

Mr. Fernandez addressed himself to the policeman. "That is the boy," he said, pointing at Angel, "who stole our baby carriage and our groceries. He lives in the house in which we live." Then he turned to his wife. "Look, Felicia, here are our groceries!"

8

"One moment, one moment," shouted Mrs. Martinez, shaking her head so that her long black earrings violently shook also. "These are not your groceries. They are mine. Here is Mr. Miraflores who can quickly say whose groceries they truly are. Mr. Miraflores, say frankly if it is or is not the cake that I bought."

Mrs. Martinez pointed a finger at the cake.

Mr. Miraflores looked into the carton and studied the chocolate cake. Then he nodded. "It is true—it is the very same cake—"

Mrs. Martinez did not wait for him to finish talking. "I have come back here to see what is happen-

ing. I have been waiting for these groceries for three hours. Sixteen relatives are coming to my house soon. Sixteen! I could not carry all the things I bought and I asked you, Mr. Miraflores, as a small favor to let your son, Carlos, bring to me the few things I could not carry."

"Carlos went with the groceries to your house, I assure you, Mrs. Martinez," said Mr. Miraflores in bewilderment, "but there has been a misunder-standing. Suddenly here is a policeman—"

"This man who is a stranger to me says my gro-ceries are his. What do you say to that?" Mrs. Martinez shouted to the policeman and talked more and more rapidly in Spanish.

Carlos and Angel stood aside, quite forgotten.

Mrs. Fernandez now ran to the policeman. "I ask you one small favor, only to listen to me!"

The policeman looked from one to another, his head moving as if he were watching a ping-pong game. He seemed more and more astonished at the new developments and at how fast Mrs. Martinez

73

could talk and how loudly Mr. Fernandez could shout.

Mrs. Fernandez was saying, "These two"—now she turned and looked for Carlos and Angel. When she caught sight of them, she pointed them out to the policeman—"these two were seen by a neighbor taking a bundle out of our house. So they must be the ones who took the baby carriage and broke it. Yes, they are the ones who broke it. It was a carriage with four wheels. Now it has only three. There are those who say the fourth was already broken, but even if it was a little bent, it was not entirely broken and entirely removed from the carriage, and all afternoon my husband has spent trying to fix the broken wheel." Mrs. Fernandez' voice was the loudest to be heard.

The policeman walked to Mr. Miraflores. He said to him, "Does this stuff belong to you?" The policeman, too, spoke in Spanish, but more slowly than the others.

"Yes," said Mr. Miraflores unhappily, "they are the groceries that Mrs. Martinez bought in my store this morning. It is actually the store of my brother, however."

"Is this your boy?"

"No, this is his friend Angel. The other one is Carlos, my son. I will soon ask Carlos where he has been, why the groceries of Mrs. Martinez have not been delivered, and why it is necessary to have a policeman find him. You may leave him to me. I know that Carlos took the groceries and disap-peared with his friend. That is bad, and Carlos knows it is bad. As you see, this lady"—Mr. Mira-flores indicated Mrs. Martinez—"needs her gro-ceries."

Mr. Miraflores called across to Carlos, "At least tell me where you have been for so long and why it is that when you are asked to deliver a carton, it is found elsewhere—"

The policeman took out his notebook once more and turned to Mrs. Fernandez. "Lady, you want to report a stolen baby carriage?" Then he translated this into Spanish for Mrs. Fernandez.

Mrs. Fernandez proved that she could speak

English. "Yes, I wish to report a baby carriage stolen."

"When did you last see the carriage, lady?"

"One moment," said Mr. Fernandez, speaking in Spanish to his wife loudly and angrily. "Felicia, it is no use to have further conversations." Then he turned to the policeman, "The baby carriage we have spoken of is at home. It is found and it is at home."

Mrs. Miraflores came forward. She said to the policeman, speaking rapidly and in Spanish also, "The carriage is found. The groceries are found. There is nothing to do now but for everyone to go home." She smiled and patted her hair.

The policeman put his notebook into his back pocket.

"Everything okay now?" The policeman looked from Mr. Fernandez to Mr. Miraflores, from Mrs. Fernandez to Mrs. Miraflores. Then he looked at Carlos and Angel.

"Everything okay," said Mrs. Miraflores, speaking English for the first time since she had arrived in New York, and again smiled at everyone and patted her shining hair.

Everything did seem much better now. Even Mr. Fernandez had stopped shouting and was only scowling. Some were laughing and others were talking to each other. The voices were friendly. The policeman walked away. The crowd began to scatter. Angel disappeared with the crowd.

Only Mr. Miraflores looked severely at Carlos. "I expect to hear an explanation. I have asked you to do one thing, only one thing. I have asked you, Carlos, to deliver a few necessities to Mrs. Martinez. What happens? A policeman arrives and there is a disturbance in front of my store. How does this happen, Carlos?"

Carlos tried to explain. "We borrowed a baby carriage—"

But Mr. Miraflores shook his head. Although he had said "How does this happen, Carlos?" he refused to listen to the explanation.

"I must tell you, Carlos, that when I ask you to bring a few groceries to Mrs. Martinez it is not necessary to have arguments and to have a crowd gather here with a policeman. I wish to tell you now, Carlos, that bad companions will lead you to disaster. Meanwhile, take the carton of groceries and bring them to Mrs. Martinez. I see she is going away as if she no longer wishes to have them."

Mrs. Martinez came hurrying back. "In all this confusion I nearly forgot the groceries. This time I will take the carton myself." She stooped and picked up the carton. "In this way I can be sure it will reach my house."

Carlos ran after her. "I will carry it for you, Mrs. Martinez. I am sorry. I can explain how this happened."

"I do not ask explanations," said Mrs. Martinez, but she let Carlos take the carton from her. "I ask only that my son and his wife and their children and my daughter and her husband and their children and my two nephews and their wives and children are not already waiting outside my door for the supper that I have not yet prepared. Also I must hurry, for I have remembered that there is a half pound of

78

chicken livers in a dish near the sink and I am hoping that my cat has not come in through the window and stolen them."

"I can run quickly, even with this carton," said
Carlos.

"Run, then! I have left the door unlocked. It is
apartment 2 B."

Carlos ran up the stairs and into Mrs. Martinez'
apartment. No one of Mrs. Martinez' family was
waiting. The window, Carlos saw, was closed. The
cat was sitting patiently outside on the fire escape.

"All is well," said Mrs. Martinez, coming into
her kitchen and looking about and seeing the closed
window and the waiting cat outside. "Thank you,
Carlos. You have given me much worry, but you
have also, at the last moment, helped me. Are
you saving money for some purpose? If so, here is
a little to add to your savings." Mrs. Martinez
searched inside her handbag and gave Carlos a
nickel.

"I will save it to buy a bicycle," said Carlos.

Mrs. Martinez shook her head and again her

earrings emphasized her feelings. "I am opposed to bicycles. Bicycles are dangerous in the crowded streets. If I were you, I would save for a sweater or a warm coat. Today is a summer day, but I have been here in New York in the winter. You may believe me, it is cold. Now, Carlos, let in the cat."

Carlos opened the window. The cat leaped into the room. Mrs. Martinez lifted the cake from the carton.

"It has the look of having been dropped," she said. "Sometimes my own cakes, the ones I myself bake also have this look. It is nothing. As long as it is good to eat, the appearance of a cake is nothing."

Mrs. Martinez smiled at Carlos. "Remember, do not buy a bicycle. It is my advice to you."

9

Although Mrs. Martinez was opposed to bicycles and had stated her reasons, the thing Carlos wanted most was a bicycle. He decided this as he walked home from Mrs. Martinez' house.

If he had a bicycle he would get a wire basket to attach to the handlebars as he had seen on some bicycles on the streets of New York. Then he could deliver groceries, or take Fernando for a ride and perhaps Paquita, also, although Paquita was almost too big for riding on handlebars. Best of all, he would ride up and down the bicycle path in Central Park.

He could ride to other places farther away, too.

He could travel all over New York if he had a bicycle.

At Ricardo's Television and Radio Repair store Carlos saw that the large television set in the corner of the store window was now turned on. A tall boy, whom Carlos had already seen in the store and had noticed in the crowd around Angel's house, leaned against the doorway. He, too, was looking at the television screen.

Carlos saw that an interesting picture was being shown. He stood watching. A criminal was escaping through a prison window. He ran down a narrow road. The alarm was set off and floodlights moved across the scene. A number of policemen on speeding motorcycles tried to capture the escaped man.

While running, the criminal himself discovered an abandoned motorcycle. One motorcycle policeman pursued him. In and out they went through narrow streets and alleys, over a high bridge, beside a river, through a tunnel. At last the prisoner had a serious accident. He ran into a stone wall but

managed to get up. He continued to run. Seeing a ladder propped against a stone wall, he climbed up.

The speeding motorcycle-policeman went so fast, he passed by the very ladder the criminal had climbed. How could the policeman now discover the hiding place of the prisoner, Carlos wondered, and stepped closer to the window.

At that moment someone inside Ricardo's Television and Radio Repair store turned the dial of the set. The picture became blurred, then faded, and was replaced by a picture of the head of a man. This man's head occupied the entire screen. The man was singing, his voice coming out of a loud-speaker on top of the doorway. He sang:

> Who needs money?
> Who needs money?
> If you need money
> General Loan is waiting for you.

Carlos understood all the words. If anyone needed money, it was himself, Carlos Miraflores, he thought. Not only did he want a bicycle, but now he also wanted a television set and a sweater or a coat for the cold weather if it was going to be as cold as Mrs. Martinez said it was in New York in winter. He felt the nickel in his pocket. He would need a hundred nickels, no, a thousand, perhaps fifty thousand nickels for all these things. How could he possibly get them? He took out the nickel and studied it. It looked very small.

The boy of Ricardo's Television and Radio Repair store went inside to adjust the television set as the picture of the man's head repeated itself, running upward on the screen. Then the boy came out again and leaned once more against the doorway.

He was a boy much taller and older than himself, Carlos observed. He wore black trousers and a pale blue shirt and his black hair was combed and shining and he was smiling. He looked a little like Museo, the baseball player.

The big boy said to Carlos from the doorway, "I am certain in that movie we have seen that in the end the criminal did not escape. Such things do not happen in the movies, but, in reality, one can often escape, especially on a motorcycle." Then he turned and walked into the store.

What the big boy said held Carlos's attention. He hoped the boy would come out again and talk to him further. Carlos waited.

In a minute or two he did come out and Carlos said, to keep him from going away at once, "A motorcycle is dangerous, I think, as you have seen in this movie. For myself I would not mind having a bicycle."

"A bicycle? Who would want a bicycle? A motorcycle such as the one we have seen, yes, I, too, would like to have, but a bicycle is like a toy. It is easy to have one, I can assure you. Are you seriously interested in having a bicycle?"

Since this big boy considered it to be a toy, Carlos was no longer certain of being interested in having one. Nevertheless he said, "A bicycle would be useful to me."

The big boy shook his head. "I can tell you much about motorcycles and bicycles, too. It happens that I am a business partner in this store. In the back we have some bicycles and parts. Call me Ricardo, by the way."

Carlos stared at the boy in astonishment. "There

are bicycles in the back of your store?"

"Yes, my friend, we have bicycles in the back and I am a partner in this business."

Not only was he a partner. The store was named for him. To be a partner in a bicycle store, and a television store also, must be the best profession there was. It was even fortunate to know someone who was a partner in a bicycle business.

Suddenly a voice called from the back of the store, "Ricardo, did you see a hammer that lay here on the bottom shelf?"

Ricardo called back, "I have borrowed it, but it is now returned and is in the tool box."

Inside his pocket Carlos held in his closed hand Mrs. Martinez' nickel. Carlos asked, "Ricardo, do you know how much a bicycle costs?"

Ricardo said, "There are many prices. A new one has a higher price, of course, than a secondhand one." Then he added in a lowered voice, "If you wish to borrow one and then return it later, that can be arranged by me as I am a partner here. And without payment." Ricardo smiled at Carlos. His teeth were very white and his smile was friendly.

Carlos was very happy. He could hardly say the words, but he managed them at last. "Yes, I would like very much to borrow a bicycle."

Someone was coming to the front of the store from the back. "Listen to me, Ricardo—" the voice said loudly, and suddenly, as if by magic, Ricardo vanished into the store, closing the door behind him.

Carlos turned away. The more he thought of Ricardo, the more interesting he became. He would have liked to hear more about the bicycle Ricardo was going to lend him. Had he, Carlos, really under' stood Ricardo about borrowing a bicycle? And "without payment"? Or had Ricardo said some' thing entirely different? When would he see him again? And when would he see the bicycles Ricardo had mentioned that were in the back of the store? Why had he, Carlos, not asked to look at them at once?

Walking home, Carlos held the nickel in his closed hand. It not only seemed very small, it felt as if it were shrinking.

10

When Carlos reached home, a worn valise made of hard brown paper was open on Uncle Jorge's bed. Into the valise Uncle Jorge was folding his few things.

"Tomorrow is Saturday and it is the day I leave," Uncle Jorge said to Carlos. "I am at last going home. Now that the day has almost arrived, I cannot believe it."

Uncle Jorge was smiling while two tears rolled down his cheeks. "I have waited a long time to go home."

Mama said, "It is arranged. Paco will go with you to the plane and then will return to us. Our neighbor, Mr. Padilla, will go along. Then Papa will not lose his way when he returns to us."

Because of Uncle Jorge's departure they did not open the grocery store the next day. The whole family and Mr. Padilla went with Uncle Jorge to the subway.

"Be good, Carlos," Uncle Jorge said to him as he was going down the steps of the subway. "Be good. As you are the oldest, teach the others to be good also. The main thing is to be good and to obey your parents and also the teacher in the big school. Then you will make something of yourself."

Uncle Jorge kissed each member of the Miraflores family.

"It is a beautiful warm day," said Mama when she could no longer see Uncle Jorge, Papa, and Mr. Padilla as they disappeared into the subway. "The store is closed. We can go to the park."

Mrs. Miraflores was wearing a red-flowered summer dress. Fernando was dressed in a white suit. Paquita wore a shining pink silk dress.

It was like a true holiday. Carlos, too, was dressed

in his best clothes, a white shirt and light green shorts.

The Miraflores family were already known in the neighborhood. Along the way to the park they met many friends.

"Hello, Mrs. Miraflores. You are not in the store, I see."

"My brother-in-law is on his way home. We have closed the store for today. Paco has taken him to the airplane."

"Hello, Paquita," a little girl called out.

"Hi, Fernando," some boys shouted.

Mrs. Miraflores said to Carlos, "It is good to have many friends. All of these friendly people are our customers. They know us and, what is more, they like us. It is true they sometimes buy their groceries at the A & P, but when they want a true Puerto Rican dinner, they come to me. They cannot find anyone in the A & P to instruct them in preparing *pasteles* such as mine. Also when our customers do not have a few dollars, I am glad to wait until the money is earned by them. They pay me a little later.

They know I do not demand to be paid before they have the money. That is why we now have good friends."

The man who sold balloons stood at the entrance to the park.

"Would you like to have a balloon, Paquita?" Mrs. Miraflores asked her.

"Yes, yes, a red one."

"And for me a green one," said Fernando.

Mrs. Miraflores made the purchase of two balloons.

"And for this one? No balloon?" asked the balloon man, pointing to Carlos.

"For me?" Carlos was astounded. "I am too old for balloons. I am more interested in a bicycle. Do you sell bicycles?"

The balloon man did not answer. He put the balloon strings on the forefingers of Fernando and Paquita.

Carlos sat with his mother on a park bench,

watching Fernando and Paquita, each on a swing, balloons flying overhead.

Carlos said, "I would like to walk toward the older boys' playground. I will soon return."

"Do not lose your way," said Mrs. Miraflores.

"I know this park," said Carlos. "I do not lose my way in it."

Carlos went down one path and up another. He saw some big boys kicking a football about and stood watching. He hoped the football, by accident, would be kicked toward him. He would kick it back, he thought, perhaps kick it higher than anyone else could. Then they would see he was a good football player and they would ask him to join the game. Although he waited for a long time, the boys did not kick the football toward him.

Carlos walked down the path toward the older children's playground, but before he reached the playground he saw that he had arrived by chance at the bicycle path.

Boys and girls and older people, too, were riding

bicycles on the bicycle path. For a time he stood watching them go by. Perhaps one would offer him a ride, or one would stop long enough so he could ask if he could borrow the bicycle for a short ride. Then, as this did not happen, Carlos continued to walk along the path toward the playground.

He looked around to see if anyone from his class was in the playground. No one he knew was there. All the swings were already taken. There was a big crowd in the ball field beyond so that he could not even see the players.

Slowly he walked away from the playground. Then he noticed someone hurrying toward him.

"We meet once more. I see you do not yet have a bicycle, Carlos." It was Ricardo. This time he was wearing a bright red shirt and white narrow trousers.

"I am glad to see you, Ricardo. It is true I do not yet have a bicycle."

"That is too bad. For myself, I am looking for a personal motorcycle. Let me show you the type of motorcycle I will have one of these days. Do you care to go for a walk?"

Carlos did not remember if he had told his mother to wait for him. He said, "Someone is waiting for me. I cannot go too far. I am going for a short walk only."

"I do not ask you to go too far. As it is a nice day, I, too, am going for a short walk. If you wish, I will show you something that will interest you. You do not wish to go with me?" Ricardo stopped suddenly. "You do not have to go with me at all if you do not wish it."

Not wish it? But it was exactly what Carlos wanted to do more than anything else. He had been lonely and here was Ricardo talking of bicycles and motorcycles. He had even promised to lend him one, if he, Carlos, had understood correctly.

"Yes, I do want to go with you, but I must soon return."

"I am glad you wish to go with me for otherwise you would miss something of great interest to you."

"Is it a bicycle?"

"It is not exactly a bicycle that I am talking about. But it is like a bicycle. If you are truly interested, we can walk there together."

"Yes, I would like to walk there."

Ricardo said, "I think you are saving up money for a bicycle. That takes a long time."

Carlos still had Mrs. Martinez' nickel in his pocket. No one else had added to his savings. He shook his head. "No, I do not think I can save up enough money for a bicycle."

"You do not have to tell me how hard it is to save money. Sometimes it is impossible. I am happy I do not have to worry. I do not think of saving money. It is good to be rich."

Carlos looked with admiration at the rich Ricardo.

"Yes, it is good to have money," said Ricardo.

They had come to the end of one path and crossed the road and walked under an overpass.

"A little way beyond you will see something that will surprise you." Ricardo stopped briefly and looked around him. "We do not wish to make a noise here. It is a quiet place."

In the brick wall were two tall, dark, wooden doors. They were the entrance to a courtyard.

Someone in dark clothing came toward Carlos and Ricardo, then turned aside, and went through an inner door. Again Ricardo stopped.

"This is a place I come to," Ricardo said, "when I have a few moments. I have brought you to the best place I know. Now I must go back to the store. Soon we will meet again." Ricardo walked quickly away.

Carlos peered through the open doors. He was truly surprised. It was just as Ricardo had said. It seemed as if a whole army of bicycles were collected in this courtyard. At the end of the courtyard there was a low, long, red brick house. Two great green lamps hung at the entrance.

Carlos looked more closely as he walked through the doors. They were not bicycles at all, but motorcycles, exactly as in the television movie he had seen. Some of these he had seen speeding through Columbus Avenue, and Broadway, too. Only now the motorcycles were not in motion. He could study them.

What Ricardo had said was true: A motorcycle

was a hundred times better than a bicycle. A motor-cycle was both stronger and larger. Carlos walked in and out among the motorcycles and saw that they were very well made. They were nothing like Miguel's frail bicycle. In that instant he decided he no longer wanted a bicycle like Miguel's but one of these.

11

Carlos stood beside the nearest motorcycle and examined it with care. He put his hands on the handlebars. They were wide apart and heavy. It was an easy matter to hold on to the handlebars and get up on the seat. Now that he was seated, he observed that the pedals were too far away from his feet. Perhaps the pedals could be moved up. If he owned this motorcycle, he would soon fix the pedals, he thought.

Carlos held on to the handlebars. He made believe he was riding down Columbus Avenue. He made a noise like a speeding motorcycle and pushed his shoulders and head forward and narrowed his eyes and smiled like Museo and Ricardo, for Ricardo, too, had a smile like Museo. Carlos was going as fast as possible on the stationary motorcycle, as fast as the escaping criminal in the television movie, as fast as the motorcycle policeman chasing the criminal.

Someone came out of a door in the low brick house and stopped a little distance away. The man stood watching. He wore a dark blue shirt and dark blue trousers.

Carlos took one hand from the handlebar and waved as if he were still riding fast down Columbus Avenue.

"Look, look," shouted Carlos, "I am going fast, no?"

"Watch the traffic," the man called back and began walking toward him.

"Okay," shouted Carlos.

When the man came closer, Carlos said, "I think I will borrow this motorcycle. You know how to start this motorcycle so it will really go?"

The man nodded.

"Okay. Show me."

The man put his hands on his hips again. "Where are you going?"

"To the store. I will put this motorcycle in the back of the store. Every morning I will go to school on it and in the afternoon I will go through the streets and I will speed. I will go to the zoo. When I go back to Paso Doble I will bring it back here. You think the place for the feet can be raised?"

"Sure."

"Then I can take it home. I do not think I can take this motorcycle home if the place for the feet is so far away. Do you know Miraflores' Grocery?"

"No."

"It is on Columbus Avenue. On each corner there is a bar. In the middle is Miraflores' Grocery. That is my uncle's grocery. I am Carlos Miraflores. For a short time we are taking care of the store. It is only until Uncle Jorge comes back. Then good-by, New York. Uncle Jorge has gone to Paso Doble which is in Puerto Rico."

The man said, "Okay. I have to leave, so you have to leave, too. See the sign? There's one outside, too."

Carlos now saw the sign. It was on the wall to the right of the motorcycles. The sign said KEEP OUT.

"I did not see the sign before," said Carlos. "I will ride away now. I will go around the park. Then I will see you again." He made the motorcycle noise again and pretended to go very fast.

"Okay, now," said the man. "You have to get out."

"Okay," said Carlos, but he did not get off.

His new friend who could fix the foot pedals was going into the low red building.

Carlos pretended to meet friends while riding on the motorcycle. "Hello, Miss Bandler," he shouted. "Hello, Papa, hello, Mama, hello, Fernando. I will soon come back to take you for a ride, Paquita. You will hold on to me. There is much room in back of me." But Angel, his friend, he did take for a ride immediately. "Hold on to me, Angel. We are going to the zoo very fast."

Now his new friend and someone else were coming out of the red building once more. They were wearing pale blue helmets. The second person, in his uniform, looked familiar. Suddenly Carlos knew who he was. He was the policeman who had seen him and Angel with the carton outside the A & P. It seemed that the policeman recognized him, too.

Carlos was astonished to see that this policeman was getting on one of the motorcycles, starting the motor and letting it run.

Over the noise of the motorcycle motor Carlos heard the first policeman say, "You still here?" From his seat on the motorcycle the policeman made going-out motions. "Okay. On the double!" he shouted to Carlos.

Carlos slipped off the motorcycle and walked out of the courtyard, hurrying a little. Underneath the KEEP OUT sign there were smaller letters. He saw the words: *Police Department.*

It was the motorcycle garage of the police. He had told one of the police he was going to take a motorcycle to his uncle's store. Perhaps now these two were on their way to the store. They would tell Papa.

As he walked under the overpass he heard the motorcycle siren, and speeding by were both police-men, the one who had been outside the A & P and his new friend.

When he came home, Papa would say, "You see, now you have shown me you wish to be bad and not good, Carlos." Papa would also say, "How can I buy you a bicycle if you are bad, Carlos?"

Mama had not waited. She had gone away from

the park bench where Carlos had left her. Fernando
and Paquita were no longer on the swings.

Carlos walked home.

Papa was there. He had opened the store on his
return home with Mr. Padilla after taking Uncle
Jorge to the plane.

Mama greeted Carlos. "You have found your way home. I did not wait for you, for I know you can find your way home now. You are already familiar with all of New York." Mama smiled at him.

Papa smiled too. "As the plane with Uncle Jorge departed I thought that in a few more weeks we, too, shall go home. New York is an astonishing place, but I will be glad to go home."

"Not I," said Carlos.

The policeman had not come to tell Papa about the motorcycle in the park. If he had come, it would have been the first thing Papa would have mentioned instead of saying he would be glad to go home soon. Carlos was very glad. Very many things were too interesting in New York to leave. The most interesting was Ricardo, who had made a remarkable promise.

12

It was now almost time to close the store. Carlos was becoming more and more certain there would be no visit from the motorcycle policeman. Carlos was sitting at a table in the back room of the store. He had written ten sentences in Spanish and translated them. It was the homework for Monday.

Miss Bandler had said, "Your handwriting is good, Carlos, but you must close all the o's." Remembering this, Carlos looked over his homework and carefully closed all the o's.

He heard the bell of the store. Then he heard a voice he thought he recognized. The door was slightly open between the room where Carlos was writing and the store. Through the opening Carlos saw Mr. Fernandez. Mr. Fernandez had some baby-carriage wheels in his hand.

Papa said, "Good evening, Mr. Fernandez. It is a fine evening. Is there something you require?"

"Yes, it is a fine warm evening," Mr. Fernandez said as if thinking of something else. Then he said, after a moment's silence, "I would like to arrange a small matter." Mr. Fernandez was scowling and was as fierce-looking as always, but tonight Mr. Fernandez did not speak in a loud voice. Carlos continued to listen to the conversation.

Mr. Fernandez said, "The carriage from which these wheels have come is no longer usable, I must inform you. In the first place, the fourth wheel is now completely broken, and it is no longer possible to repair the carriage. These three wheels, however, can be useful to you, I am certain."

"The truth is," said Papa, "I have little use for these three wheels."

"I do not ask a fantastic price for them. I might

have asked the price of an entirely new baby carriage, as I would like to replace the broken carriage, but I do not ask this. As you are in business, perhaps you will find someone who can make use of these wheels. I simply ask in exchange for them some small things, even a few groceries will be enough."

Mr. Miraflores looked doubtfully at the wheels. "What would you accept in exchange for these wheels, Mr. Fernandez?"

"A chocolate cake," said Mr. Fernandez quickly, "the same type as was given to us, then taken away. Also, possibly, two cans of garbanzo beans. These would be sufficient."

"Very well," said Mr. Miraflores, still looking doubtful, "I give you this cake and two cans of garbanzo beans in exchange for the wheels."

"I am certain these are valuable wheels, and useful ones," Mr. Fernandez said, and took the cake and the garbanzo beans without waiting for them to be wrapped. "I have already forgotten about the incident of your son and the broken carriage."

Mr. Miraflores nodded. "I am happy to hear it," he said, but he did not look happy.

"It is a fair exchange," said Mr. Fernandez. He laid the wheels on top of a case of tomato paste and turned to leave. "I almost forgot," he said, turning back. "I also require a bottle of olives and some tomato paste, two cans. You remember these, too, were in the carton given to us, then taken away."

Mr. Miraflores brought out the olives and the two cans of tomato paste. He put these into a brown paper bag. Mr. Fernandez took the bag and this time left without turning back.

When Mr. Fernandez departed, Papa came into the back room. Papa did not look at Carlos. He did not even say, "Do you wish me to think you are good or bad, Carlos?" Carlos felt worse than if he had said it.

In the morning Angel Muñoz looked into the Miraflores' Grocery to see if Carlos was ready for school. He saw that only Mrs. Miraflores was there, and came inside.

"Carlos has overslept a little," said his mother. "If you will wait one moment, he will be ready."

"Hurry up, Carlos," called Angel. "Miss Bandler does not like lateness." Angel stood waiting. While he waited, he looked around the store.

As soon as Carlos was ready, he hurried out. "I am ready, Angel."

"In one moment," said Angel. "In one moment." He lifted up and examined each of the three wheels Mr. Fernandez had left. "These are very useful wheels," he said. "And there are three."

"Hurry up," said Carlos.

On the way to school Angel said, "If we were to find a bicycle, a very old bicycle, a useless one, in fact, but one in which the steering is still good, we could make a delivery wagon. With the three wheels that are lying in your uncle's store without being used, and a steering rod and a box, a large box of wood, we can build a delivery wagon. Perhaps somewhere in the store you will find a large box that your father will give us. How much easier it would then be to deliver groceries!"

"A delivery wagon with only three wheels?"

"I will explain," said Angel. "The front half of the bicycle remains a bicycle. Then we find a box. Once we have found a box and placed it on an axle having two wheels, we have a delivery wagon."

"There are not too many deliveries to make," said Carlos. "Most of our customers carry home the things they buy."

"Even for a few—even for one—it is a big thing to have a wagon. You remember Mrs. Martinez and the carton? If we'd had a wagon then, it would have been a different story."

"Yes," said Carlos, not wanting to be reminded of it.

"There are other uses for a well-made delivery wagon. One of us can stand inside the wagon and the other one can steer. It is not only a delivery wagon then, it is also a two-passenger automobile." Angel laughed. Then he added, "It seems to me I have seen an abandoned bicycle behind the stairs in my house."

112

Carlos remembered not only Mrs. Martinez and the carton, but also the baby carriage that Angel had said was abandoned, and that had turned out to belong to the Fernandez family.

"No," Carlos said, "this time we do not take things from behind the stairs."

"I will inquire," said Angel. "Do not worry. I will be certain, first of all, that it is not a bicycle belonging to anyone."

"If a steering rod can be found that does not belong to anyone, it would be a good thing to build a delivery wagon," said Carlos. "I think I have seen a can of paint in my uncle's store. The can is already opened and the color of the paint is red."

"A red delivery wagon will be an impressive thing," said Angel.

"We could write in black paint on it: MIRA-FLORES' GROCERY," said Carlos with growing interest.

Miss Bandler, all day, had to remind both Carlos and Angel that if they had anything to say of interest to all, they could say it and not whisper to each other. They had nothing to say to the class, however.

After school Angel said good-by to Carlos at the corner.

"I will see you later if there is good news. Do not tell your father our plan. If we are successful, it will be a surprise for him. It will make him happy."

Carlos found only Mama in the store. The wheels were nowhere to be seen. "There were three wheels here on this case only this morning," said Carlos. "Did you see them?"

"Wheels? Let me remember. I saw Fernando rolling some wheels along the street. That was a long time ago, perhaps early in the morning."

Fernando was nowhere to be found.

"Paquita and Fernando went to the playground in the park," Mrs. Miraflores said. "They are with Mrs. Martinez and her grandchildren."

Carlos hurried to the playground in the park. He was happy to see that all three wheels were there. Fernando and Paquita and Maria Martinez each had one wheel. Fernando was nailing his to a box, and Paquita and Maria had the same idea. Carlos had to promise Fernando and Paquita and Maria a long ride in a new red delivery wagon before they would give up the wheels.

13

It was late in the afternoon when Carlos, carrying the three wheels, went to find Angel.

Angel was upset. "Yesterday no one wants the broken bicycle behind the stairs. Today it is valuable and belongs to everyone. The whole house—everyone I ask—says, 'This bicycle? It is mine!' They are all fighting over it. It is because I asked, 'Is this old bicycle yours?' It is better not to ask. It is better not to say, 'I would like to have this old broken bicycle.' Because I said I wanted it, it becomes valuable."

"No, it is better to ask," said Carlos. "We have already had trouble once. The bicycle is not important, after all, as we have the wheels. The most important are the wheels." But he was disap- pointed. "We will look elsewhere. We will find a way to get an old bicycle. We will look here and there. We will ask this one and that one."

Miss Bandler, the next day, looked at Carlos as his father did when he was saying, "Do you wish to be good or bad, Carlos?"

"You have not paid attention all day, Carlos. In order to learn you must pay close attention. The language is new to you. If you wish to become someone important, you will, first of all, have to learn the language well. Have you ever thought of what you would like to do when you grow up?"

"No, Miss Bandler," said Carlos.

"There are many interesting professions," said Miss Bandler. "Begin to think of this soon. It is well to think of the future, Carlos."

"Okay, Miss Bandler."

"We will talk again," said Miss Bandler. "If you have any questions about something you are interested in and wish to study, be sure you talk it over with me. You are an intelligent boy."

Carlos stopped at Ricardo's Television and Radio Repair store on his way to the park. Mr. Ortega, the owner, stood outside. Mr. Ortega had dark thick eyebrows and always seemed to be scowling.

There was nothing on the television screen.

Mr. Ortega called out, "I will turn on the tele-vision if you wish."

"Thank you. I am on my way to the playground, but I could watch for a few minutes."

"I will turn it on, then. If you wish, you may tell your father I have a few television sets that are available for renting."

"I do not think my father would be interested in renting a television set, but I will tell him. We do not have much room in our house. We live in the back of the store. It is Miraflores' Grocery."

"I have smaller sets that do not require much room. I will show you one."

Carlos stepped into the store and followed Mr. Ortega. It was his first visit inside. Perhaps he would see the bicycles and see Ricardo, too, and talk to him.

At the front of the store were the television sets, also a few sets that had been taken apart for repairs. The back of the store was dim, but Carlos could make out tools and parts of other television sets, a long-handled window pole, and, just as Ricardo had described, there were the bicycles. They were covered with dust and were placed carelessly, one against the other, beside the wall.

Mr. Ortega turned on another, smaller television set. Two ladies were seated on a swing. When Mr. Ortega turned on the sound, too, the song the ladies sang was about chewing gum.

If he were to buy a television set, Carlos thought, he would rather have the one that was in the store window and not this small one.

"Do you happen to have an old bicycle that is not of much use any longer? Or perhaps some parts of bicycles?" asked Carlos, turning away from the television sets and peering at the bicycles.

"The bicycles I have are almost new," said Mr. Ortega. He crossed his arms and went to the door of the store as if he were no longer interested in talking to Carlos. He began again looking out into the street.

Then a remarkable thing happened.

As Carlos was leaving he said to Mr. Ortega, "Where is your business partner, Ricardo, today?"

Mr. Ortega looked thunderstruck for a moment and his dark thick eyebrows rose on his forehead. Then, astonishing Carlos, Mr. Ortega burst into laughter. "My partner, Ricardo," he said while laughing, "is riding around in his automobile, of course. He is at this moment having a fine dinner at the best restaurant in New York." Then he stopped laughing. "Are you a friend of my business partner, Ricardo?"

Mr. Ortega, however, did not wait for Carlos's reply. He turned about and disappeared into the store.

Carlos did not know what to make of Mr. Ortega, but it was clear that Ricardo was too important and too rich and too busy to remember his promise. He, Carlos, would never have a bicycle to try out, it seemed, after all.

It was even difficult to make a delivery wagon which would be almost as good as a bicycle. Without a steering rod it would not be the kind of wagon that would be useful both as a delivery wagon and as a two-passenger automobile, as Angel had said. With such a wagon it might be possible to imagine —that is, if one did not look back—that one was riding a bicycle.

Someone was walking beside him.

"Hello, Carlos. I see you are again going for a walk. I will walk with you."

He was exactly the one person Carlos wanted to see again. It was Ricardo. Today Ricardo was wearing a leather jacket, although the weather was warm.

"Mr. Ortega said you were riding around today—"

"It is true. This morning I took my grandmother

to my oldest sister in the Bronx. Now I am on my way back to the store, but as I still have a few minutes, we can walk together."

Carlos was suddenly very happy. Ricardo was, after all, not too busy to walk with him.

"I have been thinking of going into a new business soon. Perhaps in a few weeks I will do so," said Ricardo.

"What kind of business is the new one?" Carlos asked, hoping Ricardo would say it was the motor-cycle business.

"This time I will have a clothing business."

"You are going to make clothing?"

Carlos already admired the clothing Ricardo had obtained for himself.

"No. It is a business of clothing that has been cleaned. To deliver this clothing I ride in an auto-mobile."

"You can drive an automobile?" asked Carlos.

"I can drive an automobile, yes, but to begin with, I will only deliver the clothing. Someone else will drive. When I am eighteen I will have my own license and a motorcycle and perhaps an automobile, too. For this I must wait three years."

Carlos was certain that in three years Ricardo would have his own license and a motorcycle and an automobile, too, just as he said. Three years seemed a short time in which to acquire so many good things.

Ricardo said, "When I have a car, I will take you for a ride. In the meantime, let us walk in the direction of the motorcycles."

"I prefer," said Carlos, remembering the KEEP OUT sign, "to walk in the direction of the bicycle path."

Ricardo stopped. Now he was laughing. "I see you still prefer a bicycle. I see I cannot convince you that a motorcycle is much better. As that is the case, however, perhaps you will want me to borrow one for you—and one for me. We will ride in the park on Saturday afternoon. At last you will see what a bicycle is really like."

"You will borrow a bicycle?"

"It is easy to do so. I have already told you that."

"And you will borrow one for me as well? Two bicycles?"

"Do not worry, I will borrow two. Do not forget I am still in the bicycle business for a few more weeks. Come to the park at one o'clock on Saturday. And let it remain our secret. Tell no one we are going for a ride. Be at the entrance to the bicycle path. Good-by, Carlos. Soon we shall meet again."

On Saturday afternoon, long before one o'clock, Carlos was waiting. He sat on a bench, then walked about, then came back to the bench and continued to wait. Ricardo did not appear. Ricardo must have forgotten his promise. Carlos watched the riders on the bicycle path, studying each one and wondering if Ricardo had gone for a ride by himself.

It seemed to Carlos he had waited for hours when, looking up, he saw Ricardo hurrying toward him. Today Ricardo wore his leather jacket again. His hair was shining, but he was not smiling.

"I am sorry, my friend was not able to let me have the bicycles for this afternoon. Another time, yes. Today, no. Next Sunday, a week from tomorrow, come again. Today I am in a hurry. I have much work." Ricardo waved and quickly walked away.

14

At school Angel said to Carlos, "My mother and father and Estrellita and the baby and I are going to Coney Island next Sunday. Do you wish to come with us? I have already told them you will come with us."

"It will be impossible," said Carlos. "On Sunday I would like to go with you but it is impossible."

"Why is it impossible?"

"There is something else I must do."

"What must you do?"

Ricardo had said, *Let it remain a secret*. After the bicycle ride he could tell Angel everything, but not now. "I cannot tell you yet. Later, yes."

125

Miss Bandler said, "If there is something of interest you wish to say, tell it to all of the class, but do not whisper."

This time Ricardo was already waiting when Carlos came to the bicycle path. There were the bicycles, one dark blue and one dark green. They were not new, but there was only a little rust on the fenders. One had a large shining bell on the handlebar and this one Ricardo gave to Carlos to ride.

"If you are not yet experienced as a bicycle rider," said Ricardo, "I will teach you."

Before he went out on the bicycle path, Carlos got up on the bicycle. He immediately fell off, then tried again. Again he fell off. The third time he was more cautious, balanced himself carefully, and stayed on.

"You learn quickly," said Ricardo, watching Carlos. Ricardo was smiling. Carlos nearly fell off again, hearing Ricardo praise him.

Together they went down the bicycle path, Ricardo leading. His hair was shining and he wore a red handkerchief around his neck. With the pale blue shirt, today he wore new black trousers. Today Ricardo smiled often.

Suddenly it was easy. After the careful balancing of the first few minutes, Carlos felt as if he had been riding a bicycle all his life.

He looked cautiously to one side, then to the other. He hoped someone from his class would see him, particularly he wished Angel were there. Now he would be happy to be seen by Angel. It would explain why he had not been able to go to Coney Island. He no longer regretted not going with the Muñoz family. Coney Island could be visited another Sunday, but the bicycle ride was available only today, when Ricardo had offered it.

Carlos thought he saw Felipe Solero. He would have waved, but he did not trust himself to take one hand off the handlebars.

They continued to ride on the bicycle path. The muscles in the back of Carlos's legs began to ache, but the aching was nothing compared to the pleasure of riding on a bicycle.

Ricardo went ahead swiftly, then slowed down and circled about Carlos. Carlos attempted to circle also, but felt himself falling. He continued in a straight line. Then he tried lifting the hand from the right handlebar. It was easy. He steered only with his left hand. Then he tried to lift both hands away, and only by quick thinking and balancing stopped himself from falling. He put both hands back on the handlebars.

It was cool. The breeze turned into a light wind. Carlos hoped this ride could go on forever. No matter how tired his leg muscles were, he could easily disregard them.

Ricardo circled and came alongside Carlos. "It is time to turn back," Ricardo said.

"Okay," said Carlos, but what he wanted to say was, "Not yet, please."

"You can imagine now," said Ricardo, "how much better it is to ride on a motorcycle. There is no work to riding on a motorcycle. Your muscles do not get tired on a motorcycle."

Carlos, however, could not think of anything that

would be better. He said, "This is the best ride I have ever had in all my life."

At the park entrance Ricardo said, "Okay, Carlos. Now I must take back your bicycle to my friend from whom I have borrowed it, and mine also."

"I will be happy to walk it there with you," said Carlos.

"No, as I borrowed these myself, I will now return them myself." Ricardo was smiling. "Good-by, Carlos. Soon we will meet again."

"Good-by, Ricardo." Carlos watched him guide both bicycles. "Thank you very much, Ricardo."

"It is nothing," said Ricardo over his shoulder.

15

It was growing dark. It had been a long ride, but to Carlos it had seemed a matter of minutes. It was true his legs ached as if he had run for miles. He felt, too, as if he were still on the bicycle, and his feet felt as if they were pedaling and walking at the same time.

Carlos saw that Mama and Papa were both standing at the door of the store looking anxiously toward him as he approached. Mama even came to meet him.

"Where were you, Carlos? What were you doing? You did not ride on a bicycle, is that not true?"

131

Carlos was surprised. How could they know about the bicycle ride?

Papa said, "Come inside."

Carlos followed his father into the store. Mama walked behind him. Papa shut the door. Papa looked as if he were saying, "Do you wish to be considered good, Carlos, or bad?" No, he looked as if he were saying, "Now I see you wish to be considered bad, Carlos." But Papa said nothing.

Mama repeated, "You did not ride on a bicycle, Carlos. I cannot believe you have been riding on a bicycle, as we have been told."

"It is true I had a ride on a bicycle," said Carlos.

"On a *bicycle*?" asked Papa as if a bicycle was as dangerous and unusual to ride as a tiger.

"My friend, Ricardo, borrowed one for himself and one for me. We took the bicycles into the park and we went for a ride on the bicycle path."

Suddenly Mama began to cry. "Do not be alarmed, Carlos," Mama said through her tears, "if the policeman comes here and asks for you. Do not be alarmed." Carlos was at once alarmed, but it was clear, also, that she herself was greatly alarmed.

"Where did you find this Ricardo?" asked Papa. "He is not a boy from your school."

This made Mama cry even more.

"Once you are one of a gang of lawbreakers, they will lead you to disaster," said Papa.

"Ricardo is not one of a gang," said Carlos. "He borrowed a bicycle for himself and one for me. We took a ride—only we two. That is all that has happened." It was very difficult to keep himself from crying, however, as Mama was crying.

"Now I will tell you what this Ricardo means by 'borrowing,'" said Papa. "A little while ago Mr. Ortega comes to us and says he is going to the police station. 'Why are you going to the police station?' Mama asks him. 'Two bicycles are missing from the back of my store,' says Mr. Ortega, 'and I have information as to who is riding on those bicycles. One of these is Carlos, your son.'

"Mr. Ortega tells us that you are a friend of this Ricardo who works in his store. It is true?"

"Ricardo is a business partner of Mr. Ortega."

"You hear that, Rosa? Mr. Ortega already told us that you think Ricardo is his partner. It is Ricardo's desire to impress you and you believe him although he is a boy who only cleans up the store."

"I have met him there. We talked together," said Carlos.

"What did you talk about? About gangs?" asked Papa.

"About bicycles," said Carlos.

"Mr. Ortega told us that Ricardo has a habit of borrowing—once it is tools, once a hammer, then this, then that. Today he has decided to borrow two bicycles. This is not borrowing. It is stealing, says Mr. Ortega. You have been riding on a stolen bicycle, Carlos."

"It did not look like a stolen bicycle."

"A stolen bicycle has the appearance of any other bicycle, Carlos. Mr. Ortega says someone told him you have been seen riding in the park. On the bicycle path."

"Ricardo will return the bicycles. I left him a few minutes ago. He told me he was taking them back to the place where he got them."

Papa shook his head. "Ricardo will not return the bicycles, I can assure you. As you have been riding on a stolen bicycle, you, too, have done a bad thing. We will try to explain all of this, but we cannot help what others think. And I will tell you something else. There is a policeman waiting for Ricardo. In his house."

"I will go then," said Carlos. "I can explain to Mr. Ortega that if he will wait the bicycles will soon be there."

"I will explain if it is necessary," said Mama.

Papa said, "Stay here, Carlos. It is better for you not to see this Ricardo again."

This was worse than saying he had been riding on a stolen bicycle. "Ricardo is my friend," Carlos said.

A little girl came into the store. She bought a quart of milk and two avocados.

Two old ladies followed her and stood talking together. Mama hastily dried her eyes. The ladies looked sympathetically at Mama. One of them asked for a box of starch, which Mama put into a brown paper bag.

When they left she said, "I will give you your

supper, Carlos. Call Paquita and Fernando. I will give you all your supper now. Find the children, Carlos. They are playing nearby. But do not go away. Only find them and return here."

Carlos went out of doors.

Paquita was bouncing a ball, but Fernando was at the corner.

"Get Fernando, Paquita," said Carlos. "It is suppertime. I will wait here for you."

Paquita ran down the block while Carlos stood waiting.

Nearby a young woman said to an older one who was seated on a folding chair on the sidewalk, "The ambulance has already come. They have taken away the boy. He has been hurt and it was because of the bicycles. The truck collided with the bicycles and the boy fell. I saw that he was unconscious."

Carlos's heart began to bang against his chest.

"I am sorry for the grandmother," said the old lady. "It is she who has brought him up and worked for him. Without him, what will she do? He was her hope."

"I did not say he is dead. I simply said he was unconscious."

"But who knows if he will live?"

Who knows if he will live. . . . The words frightened Carlos. He felt he had to run away from these words. He began to run in the direction of the hospital, three blocks away. It was surely Ricardo they were talking about. It was Ricardo who was hurt. He had to see him. He had to tell everyone, especially Mr. Ortega who did not understand that Ricardo had only borrowed the bicycles.

Now, almost at the hospital, Carlos stopped and then walked slowly. If he had not told Ricardo that he wanted a bicycle ride, Ricardo would not have borrowed one and not been hurt. Perhaps Ricardo was dead. If Ricardo was dead, it was because of him, Carlos.

16

Carlos hurried into the wide, quiet hall of the hospital.

A young lady sat at the desk. On the top of her dark head a tiny white cap looked as if it would fall off if she turned her head.

"My friend Ricardo," Carlos said quickly, "I would like to see him. I would like to find out if he is okay."

The lady turned her head. The cap did not fall off. "What is your friend's name?"

"Ricardo."

"Ricardo? Ricardo what? What is the second name?"

138

He had never asked Ricardo his whole name. "I do not know. He has been in an accident and his name is Ricardo," Carlos repeated.

"I will try to find out about your friend. I will call Emergency," the lady said, and smiled at Carlos. She turned to the telephone and talked in a low voice. Then she said to Carlos, "There have been many accidents today. Without a second name it is difficult. I can tell you this: There have been no serious accidents today."

"He is alive? You are sure Ricardo is alive? Let me talk to him, please. It is very important. There is something I have to tell him."

The nurse talked into the telephone again. Then she said to Carlos. "There was one Ricardo this afternoon. His name is Ricardo Antillas. If it is he, he is already out of danger. Children, however, are not allowed in the ward. Do not worry. I have told you there have been no serious accidents today. If he is in this hospital and has come today to Ac- cidents or Emergency, and if he is Ricardo Antillas, it is not serious."

140

If he is in this hospital? It had not even occurred to Carlos that there were other hospitals.

He walked home quickly. He would have to stop to talk to Mr. Ortega. He would have to explain that it was his own fault about the borrowed bicycle. He would explain, then Mr. Ortega would go to the hospital and tell Ricardo he did not blame him.

He had left, he remembered, only to get Paquita and Fernando into the house for supper. But he had to see Mr. Ortega at once. He began to run; then as he reached Ricardo's Television and Radio Repair store he saw it was closed.

He continued to run home, expecting Mama and Papa to demand where he had been. Instead they were inside the store and an old lady, very small and bent and white-haired, was sitting on a stool and fanning her face with a paper bag.

She said to Carlos the moment he came in, "They have told me you were the one to go with Ricardo." Then she nodded sadly. "Now he is in the hospital. They said to me at the hospital, 'Go home. All is well with him. Tomorrow you may come. Today, no.' But if all is well with him, why may I not see my own grandson?"

Mama said, "It is the habit to tell bad news at once, so the news is, at least, not bad. Your grandson must regain his strength. It is better that he rests and there are no visitors. Even his grandmother must not be nearby. That is the rule of the hospital, I have heard. Here is a cold drink. Do not worry. Your grandson is alive, Mrs. Antillas; you must be grateful for this."

"I am grateful that he is alive, it is true." Ricardo's grandmother nodded at Carlos. She stood up. She was very small even standing up. "I will go home. If it is true that I may visit Ricardo tomorrow, I will make the *pasteles* he likes. I will pray and I will make the *pasteles*. Good-by. You have been kind." She turned to Carlos. "I have heard everything. Do not think I blame you, Carlos. You are innocent."

Mama said, "I will walk to your house with you."

When they left, Carlos said to his father, trying not to cry, "I know that Ricardo was on his way to

142

return the bicycles. He told me this. He did not steal them."

Papa said a surprising thing. "I believe you, Carlos. It is not that I do not believe you, Carlos. It is the policeman who must believe you. And this I do not know. It is late. Eat your supper. It is waiting for you. And go to sleep. Tomorrow we will see what can be done."

Carlos could not fall asleep.

He lay shivering with cold, although the evening was warm. It seemed to Carlos it was the middle of the night when he heard the store bell ring.

"Perhaps you can answer a few questions," said a voice in Spanish, a man's voice. "I must tell you that your boy is concerned in this. Ricardo Antillas has taken property that does not belong to him and your son was in this theft, also."

Carlos lay listening and trembling.

It was Mama's voice that answered. "I have talked with this boy's grandmother, Mrs. Antillas. I know that this boy is not a thief. She has told me that perhaps he likes to make believe he is already a man

143

and can grant favors to others. But a thief, no."

The man's voice said, "It is not a question of your belief. Or of his grandmother's. It is a question of the facts."

Carlos's fright and trembling increased. He felt cold. His throat and mouth were dry.

Mama said, "I am telling you the facts."

Despite his fright, Carlos was surprised. Mama was not crying now. She sounded as if she were smiling. "Ricardo wishes to show the younger boy, Carlos, my son, that if it is a question of borrowing a bicycle to ride on, he can do this favor for him. He wants to show Carlos he is already an important man."

"It is a question of two bicycles, I must remind you," corrected the man. "And both bicycles are now broken. Who can be responsible if not Ricardo Antillas and, I must add, your son, also?"

"I do not say they are not to blame. That is another matter. I say it is not a question of stealing. It is not in Ricardo's nature. I have heard this from his grandmother."

144

"What his grandmother says is not exactly the fact."

"Excuse me, I believe it is the fact. Who knows a child better than his grandmother?"

"I believe a grandmother may know a child, but may not state the fact correctly. She may wish to be protective."

"This grandmother states the facts honestly and simply. I have sent my husband to talk to Mr. Ortega. I think it would be well to talk to Mr. Ortega to discover what his opinion is. As they are his bicycles, and as Ricardo has worked for him, he is the one who can give much information."

"Mr. Ortega?"

"Yes, his store is nearby. It is an easy matter to talk to him if you wish. I am certain he does not consider Ricardo a thief."

"Excuse me, Mrs. Miraflores, but it is Mr. Ortega himself who has said the bicycles were stolen from him."

"Ah, yes, perhaps that was before he knew of the accident. He did not know that at the very moment he was complaining about Ricardo's taking the bicycles, the bicycles were on their way to him. Unfortunately the accident happened, and the truck destroyed the bicycles. What can one do?"

The man's voice said slowly and carefully, as if explaining this to a young child instead of to Mama, "But even borrowing is a bad thing. Especially when one does not say frankly, 'I am borrowing two bicycles.' "

"Ah, now I agree," said Mama. "It is wrong not to explain, but that is all. It is only a question of stating in advance, 'I would like to borrow something.' But then consider what might have happened if he had asked Mr. Ortega. Mr. Ortega might have said, 'No, Ricardo. I do not wish you to borrow the bicycles.' And Ricardo could not then show Carlos that Ricardo is a person of some importance."

"If Ricardo would not have borrowed the bicycles, they would not now be wrecked. Would not Mr. Ortega have been better off?"

"But this has already happened. How can one say, 'If he would not have taken the bicycles?' He did take them. It is unfortunate. It was wrong and it turned out badly. Yet I say Ricardo is not a thief."

Carlos opened the door a crack. He saw that the man wore a dark blue uniform.

"I am going back to the station now with all you have told me, Mrs. Miraflores, in my notebook. It is not up to me, I hope you will understand. It is up to the court. Ricardo must still reply to Mr. Ortega's complaint."

Carlos went back to bed and almost at once was asleep. At least Mama was not angry. She no longer was crying. He had not known there could be so much trouble because of one bicycle ride. But at least Mama believed Ricardo was not a thief.

17

Carlos awoke very early in the morning. He had formed a plan almost as he slept. He would go to see Mr. Ortega to convince him that Ricardo was returning the bicycles to his store when the accident happened. Without telling anyone, he would go to Mr. Ortega. He, Carlos, alone knew it was Ricardo's intention, for Ricardo had told him so.

While Carlos was eating his breakfast all that had happened seemed as if it had happened only in his dream. No one referred to yesterday. Papa only looked unhappily at him. Mama said no more than, "Eat, Carlos. Are you not going to wait for Angel

148

this morning?" as she saw him hurrying out.

"No, I will go to school early this morning," he said. But approaching Mr. Ortega's store, he saw the door was still closed. A lock hung on the door. He would have to see Mr. Ortega later, then, perhaps on the way home. Surely the store would be open then.

Miss Bandler, too, seemed not to be friendly today. In the afternoon, when it was almost time to go home, Miss Bandler said, "Carlos, please stay for a few minutes after the class is dismissed."

He had not once whispered today to Angel. Could Miss Bandler have heard about the bicycles, too?

After the class had gone out, Miss Bandler at once said, "Carlos, someone has come to the school during the day to ask about you. I have given him a good report. Now you must tell me your side of it. What happened?"

"I will tell you, Miss Bandler. I went for a ride with my friend, Ricardo, who borrowed a bicycle for me. Then while returning it, he had an accident."

Miss Bandler said, "Carlos, it is better if I know the truth. I must tell you the person who came was a policeman. Try to remember if Ricardo said it was a borrowed bicycle, or one he owned. Try to remember if he said he would return it."

"He said he would return it. I asked if I could walk it back and he said, 'As I borrowed these myself, I will now return them myself.' "

"Those were his words?"

"Yes, Miss Bandler. Now I would like to hurry home because I would like to find out if Ricardo is better. Later I must speak to Mr. Ortega."

"I can reassure you, Carlos. Ricardo is much better. I must tell you, too, that there is a charge against him of stealing bicycles."

"That is why I must speak to Mr. Ortega. He is the one who owned the bicycles."

Miss Bandler said an astonishing thing. "I would like to come with you, Carlos, to see Mr. Ortega. May I?"

"Okay, Miss Bandler," Carlos said. He could not tell Miss Bandler how happy he was suddenly, to have her come with him to call on Mr. Ortega.

It was puzzling. Miss Bandler did not ask questions. Miss Bandler talked of other things, while walking, than of Ricardo and the bicycles. It was as if they were going to the zoo or for a walk on Columbus Avenue. It was as if Miss Bandler knew very well how many worries Carlos had and did not wish to add to them.

Miss Bandler said, "I think it is beginning to rain. Yes, I have felt a few drops. It seems to me that when I take my umbrella it is a guarantee that it will not rain. Carlos, have you ever seen snow?"

"No, Miss Bandler."

"You have a very wonderful experience, then, ahead of you. Wonderful and beautiful, as you will see next winter."

"I do not think I will be here next winter."

"Does that make you glad, that you will not be here next winter?"

He began to say, "Yes, Miss Bandler," and discovered it would not be true. "No, Miss Bandler, I would like to see snow. I would like to be here next winter."

Together, Carlos and Miss Bandler turned the

corner. Miss Bandler said, "You will be glad to know that Ricardo is already out of the hospital and is now at home."

Everything had seemed hopeless a few minutes before. Now that Ricardo was out of the hospital and Miss Bandler was walking beside Carlos and telling him this and smiling, everything was changing. The hope began to grow that even Mr. Ortega would listen and be reasonable and believe him.

Mr. Ortega, however, did not seem at all reasonable.

As Miss Bandler and Carlos came into his store Mr. Ortega drew down his fierce eyebrows and scowled at Carlos. A brass band was being shown on the television screen in the window and loud music was issuing into the street. Mr. Ortega at once turned off the picture and the music.

"So you have come to see me," he said to Carlos, "you who are the great friend of Ricardo." Mr. Ortega scowled at Miss Bandler, too.

"Wait, Mr. Ortega," said Miss Bandler. "We

wish to explain something. I am Miss Bandler, a schoolteacher. I know both Ricardo Antillas and Carlos Miraflores."

"Even before you make explanations, let us go to the back of the store, Miss Bandlera," said Mr. Ortega, and hastily led them past the television sets, large and small, past the radio parts and heaped-up wires and tools.

Mr. Ortega pulled a string and a single electric light shone on some twisted wire wheels and two bent handlebars and steering rods, one green and one blue. Carlos saw the large shining bell that had been attached to the bicycle he had been riding. His

heart sank. The bell was the only thing that was as good as it had been before the accident.

"You see, Miss Bandlera, this is the result of the kindness of Ricardo to his friend, Carlos Miraflores. Who is to pay for this? These were new bicycles. These were *almost* new bicycles."

Miss Bandler did not begin her explanations at once. She said, "There will have to be payment made for these. You will not be expected to take this loss. Let me assure you of that at once."

Mr. Ortega looked at Miss Bandler as if he did not believe her.

Miss Bandler said, "I have discovered the fault was also on the part of the truck driver. I have spoken to the policeman and I have seen the report of the accident. Also the insurance of the truck will repay you for both bicycles. You do not have to worry about payment. It is about the punishment of Ricardo that I have come to talk to you."

"These bicycles will be paid for?" asked Mr. Ortega lifting his eyebrows high on his forehead.

"Yes, you will receive the value of the bicycles."

"You are certain of this?" asked Mr. Ortega.

"I am certain. It is not my habit to make a promise without being certain." Miss Bandler took from her handbag a folded paper. "This is the truck company's statement." She read to Mr. Ortega: "Value of two bicycles to be stated by Ricardo Ortega and paid by the undersigned. . . ." She handed him the paper.

"Whatever I will write will be paid?"

"If it is not unreasonable."

"I am not an unreasonable man. Do you think I am an unreasonable man?" asked Mr. Ortega.

"I hope you are not," said Miss Bandler.

"No, I am not." Mr. Ortega wrote something, then crossed it out, then wrote something else, and crossed that out. Then wrote again.

"You are certain now?" asked Miss Bandler.

"Yes, I will be paid enough if I receive fifty dollars."

"I am almost certain you will be paid fifty dollars

for the two secondhand bicycles. I have been told that Ricardo has worked for you for over a year," Miss Bandler added.

"It is true, and I do not complain about Ricardo's work. It is Ricardo's nature I complain of. This boy —I am certain he has promised this boy"—he pointed his finger at Carlos—"that he would lend him a television set and a radio and tools also. Ricardo is very generous but he is generous with *my* tools and *my* bicycles. Is it not true that he has promised you these things?" Mr. Ortega now asked Carlos.

"No," said Carlos. "He did not promise any of these things. He said he would borrow a bicycle only. It is true we rode on the borrowed bicycles, but when he left me at the park he said he was on his way to return them. He was on his way here, to this store, when the accident happened."

"Mr. Ortega," said Miss Bandler, "when Ricardo borrowed tools, did he return them?"

Mr. Ortega said, "It is true that when Ricardo borrowed tools he returned them. Sometimes he removed the rust and oiled them, also, when he returned the tools. I do not deny this. But it is also true that if he had asked to borrow two bicycles, I would surely have refused."

"I would like only one thing," said Miss Bandler. "When you are asked again—and I have requested the policeman to ask you again—if you think that Ricardo *stole* the bicycles, you will say again what you have just said to me. Only say to the policeman, 'When Ricardo borrowed tools, he returned them.' Mr. Ortega, I have brought you good news about the insurance. Perhaps in return you will make this promise."

"I am glad to make this promise, Miss Bandlera."

"Miss Bandler," she said.

"Miss Bandler," said Mr. Ortega.

"Good-by, Mr. Ortega," said Miss Bandler.

"Good-by, Miss Bandlera," said Mr. Ortega.

18

Carlos had been home from school only a few minutes the next day, when old Mrs. Antillas came shuffling and hurrying into the Miraflores' Grocery.

"Ricardo has asked me to come here. Ricardo is almost well. But I have come for another reason also. The reason I have come is to ask you to visit Ricardo, Carlos. He wishes to tell you something. At the same time I invite you to a little celebration, for I am thankful that Ricardo is alive and not killed by the truck. I am thankful also that the man of the bicycle store now believes that Ricardo did not intend to steal his bicycles. For these reasons we will have a little celebration.

"Perhaps you, too, Mr. and Mrs. Miraflores, will visit us. Your little children are welcome, also. My neighbor, Mrs. Montez, has come here and has already bought the things for the celebration."

"As you see," said Mama, "we cannot leave our store, but we wish you happiness."

"I must tell you," said Papa, "that Carlos and my wife, Rosa, have convinced me about Ricardo. I do not think now as I once thought, that Ricardo wishes to be bad and not good."

Mrs. Antillas said, "I trust my heart. My heart tells me Ricardo is good. There are those who are bad and those who are good and Ricardo is of the good ones. I have seen this from childhood in him." Mrs. Antillas was so small that she had to look up at Carlos. Mrs. Antillas said this while looking up at Carlos.

"Can you go now to visit Ricardo?" It was Papa speaking. "He will be happy to see you and to hear of your visit with the teacher, Miss Bandler, to

Mr. Ortega. I have heard about that visit from Mr. Ortega. He, too, does not think bad things of Ricardo, Mrs. Antillas." Only yesterday Papa had forbidden him, Carlos, to see Ricardo again.

"I will come to see Ricardo, Mrs. Antillas," said Carlos, "in one hour. Perhaps in less than one hour."

Carlos looked for the number of Ricardo's house that his grandmother had left. Ricardo had said, "It is good to be rich," pretending that he was rich, but he lived in a house even older and more crowded than the house in which Angel and the Fernandez family lived.

Ricardo and his grandmother lived on the top floor. Carlos was breathless when he reached the last landing. The door stood open. Carlos saw at once that he was not the only one who had come to the celebration. Several neighbors and their children were there—and Miss Bandler!

Miss Bandler sat in an armchair. Because she was not wearing her eyeglasses, she looked different. She was wearing a rose-colored summer dress with silver

160

ribbons and there was a silver ribbon around her hair.

She saw Carlos and waved to him, and when she did so, she looked as Mama did when she saw Carlos coming down the street, pretty and happy and pleased to see him.

Ricardo, however, looked altogether changed. Lying on a couch with a pale blue cover over him, he now seemed to be fifteen years old and not, as usual, entirely grown up.

"Hello, Carlos," he called, not loudly as always. Only his smile was the same, wide and cheerful.

"How do you feel, Ricardo?" asked Carlos.

"Now I am okay."

Carlos said, "I am sorry about the bicycles, Ricardo. It was my fault."

"No, it was certainly not your fault, Carlos. I must tell you I have not always told the truth to you. Now you know I was not a business partner of Mr. Ortega and it was not my store. It was only that Mr. Ortega's name is Ricardo also. It is his name and not mine that is on the sign on the store. I thought you would believe it was my store. I think you believed it."

"It does not matter," said Carlos. "I am glad you have not been badly hurt in the accident."

"If I did not have the accident, Miss Bandler would not now be visiting us. I would not have made the decision I have made."

Miss Bandler said, "You can tell Carlos your decision."

"I am going back to school, Carlos. I left Miss Bandler's class last year because I thought it would be better and more impressive to have a job. I have decided I can do this job after school if I will work a little harder. A few more hours of work every day after school will not hurt me."

"In the clothing business, Ricardo?"

"No, I am going back to Mr. Ortega. He has asked me to come back."

"I am glad," said Carlos, feeling happy, seeing himself and Angel and Ricardo walking to school together, and walking home together, too, from school, and talking together in the playground.

Miss Bandler said, "Every good profession requires a person to be educated. Both of you, Ricardo and Carlos, too, should now begin to think of professions."

"I have already decided," said Ricardo. He was smiling and now he looked as always, almost grown up.

"Tell us," Miss Bandler said, and she, too, was smiling.

"I will go to school as I have said. I will learn as much as I can. I will then take the examinations that are necessary to become a motorcycle policeman. It is my ambition."

Carlos stared at Ricardo in amazement. It seemed exactly right for Ricardo to be a motorcycle policeman. Ricardo had said it with so much confidence that it was as if Ricardo were already a motorcycle policeman.

"You have made a wise decision," said Miss Bandler. "I believe you will accomplish your ambi-

164

tion. If one wants to do something very much, it is more than possible that one succeeds."

Ricardo's grandmother brought in a large plate with a cake on it. It was already cut into thin slices. It was a cake that Carlos recognized. Each day three such cakes were delivered to Miraflores' Grocery, and each day all three were sold. It was the most desirable of the cakes in the Miraflores' Grocery store. Because they were so desired by the customers, Carlos had not yet tasted this cake.

Mrs. Antillas greeted Miss Bandler as if she were her oldest and best friend. "Please, eat a piece of cake," said Mrs. Antillas. "You shall be the first."

Miss Bandler said to Mrs. Antillas, "It is good to be here and to share this cake and this celebration. You will be happy to hear that your grandson intends to become a motorcycle policeman."

To Mrs. Antillas, too, it was as if Ricardo had already become a motorcycle policeman. She looked at him with the respect a motorcycle policeman should receive, and then turned to Miss Bandler. "It is you I must thank for this. I have begged

Ricardo to return to school, but until today he has refused."

The neighbors, their children, Miss Bandler, Carlos, Mrs. Antillas, and Ricardo all ate the cake and drank papaya juice that had come from two tall cans. It was truly an exceptional cake, Carlos thought.

Miss Bandler and Carlos walked home together after the celebration. Carlos was thinking that in a few weeks he would be leaving not only Miss Bandler but Ricardo, too. It was a sad thought after the happy afternoon. If he would not have to return to Puerto Rico, if he could stay in New York, what would he do? A curious thing occurred to him.

He was imagining it was many years from now and he, Carlos, would be escaping. He did not know exactly from where, but he was on a motorcycle and escaping. There would be a chase and the motorcycle policeman who would catch him would be Ricardo. Ricardo would recognize him and say, *You are my old friend, Carlos. I will let you go free. I will not arrest you.* It was as real as if he saw it happening on a television screen. Carlos and Ricardo, a story of two friends, one a criminal and one a motorcycle policeman.

He looked up at Miss Bandler and she looked down at him. He was embarrassed at what he had been imagining. It was as if he were still thinking that he would be a bad guy when he grew up.

"What are you thinking, Carlos?" Miss Bandler said. "Perhaps you, too, have come to a decision. Today is a day of decisions. Perhaps you, too, know what you will do when you grow up."

Carlos said hurriedly, "I think if I would stay in New York and not go back to Puerto Rico, I would like to be one of those I have seen in the television stories."

"You would like to be an actor, Carlos? A television actor?"

"Yes, Miss Bandler." It was better to say this than to say he had been thinking of being a criminal.

"And perhaps to make up the stories, too?"

That would be much better. He could think of

167

many stories about people like Uncle Jorge who went home, happy and shedding tears at the same time, and about Ricardo who was going back to school because he had a great ambition, and Estrellita who could find anything that was lost. Especially he could tell the story about someone like Miss Bandler, a teacher who could understand people like Ricardo and matters like the borrowed bicycles.

"Yes, that is what I would like to do if I stay in New York, Miss Bandler. I would like to make up stories."

"It is something one can do anywhere," said Miss Bandler.

"I would prefer to be here," said Carlos, thinking that all the stories began here, with Ricardo and Miss Bandler. He would not like to leave them now that they were his friends whom he knew well.

"I have told Ricardo and now I tell you that whatever you wish to do very much is not too difficult to accomplish."

To make up stories and even to act in them did not seem difficult to accomplish. He wished now he could stay in New York. He wished he could show Miss Bandler he could become an actor, a very good actor, and appear on television, and write the words for all the other actors.

"Good-by, Carlos, I will see you tomorrow."

"Good-by, Miss Bandler."

19

Although a light rain was steadily falling, it was a beautiful day, thought Carlos. A great
many people knew him, and everyone knew Mama
by this time.

"Hello, Carlos," someone called. It was the oldest
grandchild of Mrs. Martinez.

"Carlos—hello—" called Estrellita from down the
block. "Is everything okay?"

"Everything is now okay," called back Carlos.

Papa looked up when he came into the store, and
Papa was smiling. "Mr. Ortega is a different person
since Miss Bandler visited him. He is friendly. It is as

though he does not mind anymore if one borrows from him. He has come with a small television set. 'Keep it,' he said to me, 'for thirty days. It is free. Then, if you do not wish it any longer, return it and there will be no cost.' I had to refuse. I am afraid that if I have a television set for thirty days, I will continue to want it. And for this, much money is needed."

Mama came in from the street. She looked worried. In her hand was a letter. "I have met the postman with this letter. He called it Special Delivery. Please—" She handed it to her husband as if not wanting to be the first to read bad news.

Papa hastily opened the envelope. "Uncle Jorge writes:

Dear Brother and Sister and little children, Perhaps you will not mind if I ask a great favor of you. Will you offer the store for sale? I must tell you I do not think I will return to New York again. I am now too old. Whatever you will receive for it, I will be glad if you will share with me when you return here, but I have thought and talked with my children and

171

even my grandchildren. They do not wish me to return. The truth is I truly wish to remain here for,
besides the children, I remember the winters of New
York and I do not like snow and the bitter cold. I
am sorry to put so great a burden on you, but do not
worry if the price you are offered is not high."

Mama's eyes were filled with tears, but also she
looked happy.

Papa looked at her, then at Carlos.

"I am wondering," said Papa, "if our family truly
wishes to return to Paso Doble when we have sold
the store for Uncle Jorge. What do you say, Rosa?"

"For me, I find New York is an exceptional
place," said Mama. "I prefer to stay here. If you,
Paco, do not prefer to stay, we can go back, of
course." She smiled at Papa, the tears making her
eyes bright, and patted her hair. Then Mama looked
at Carlos.

"I too prefer to stay," said Papa. "We can our-
selves be the buyers of Uncle Jorge's store. We can
be the owners of Miraflores' Grocery store. The
name is the same. We can buy it not at once, but
we can pay Uncle Jorge a little at a time. I think

he will be happy to know we are continuing the Miraflores business." He too was looking at Carlos as he said this. Then he said, "Carlos, do you prefer to stay or to go home?"

"To stay, absolutely to stay," said Carlos.

From the other room came Fernando's voice. "I prefer to stay—" The lisp had gone, now that the new teeth had grown in.

Paquita came into the store. She was smiling. "I do not wish to leave my school and my teacher— I do not wish to leave New York at all."

Carlos had to tell someone. He had to tell Ricardo and Miss Bandler and Angel. Of these, Angel was nearest. As Carlos was going out he saw a pair of handlebars with a steering rod attached and a shining silver bell on the handlebars. He recognized it. The steering rod was only a very little bit bent. It could easily be straightened.

"How does this happen to be here?" Carlos asked his father.

"As I told you, Mr. Ortega was here. He told me you were looking for a steering rod with handlebars attached. It is part of one of the two bicycles that Ricardo borrowed. It is the one that is the least damaged and it is yours if you want it. That is what Mr. Ortega said."

"I will show it to Angel," said Carlos, picking up the steering rod with its handlebars and bell. I will ask his opinion."

He had much good news for Angel. As he hurried to Angel's house he met Mr. and Mrs. Fernandez and Rosita taking a walk. Rosita was now walking by herself and had no need of a carriage.

"Hello, Carlos," called Mr. and Mrs. Fernandez as if there had never been a misunderstanding over a baby carriage.

"Hello, everyone," Carlos called back.

"Look, Angel—" Carlos said when he arrived, out of breath, and showed him the steering rod with its attachments.

"It is yours, Carlos? It is perfect! Now we can build a delivery wagon. This bar is only a little bit bent. We can easily straighten it. As Mr. Fernandez

174

has just gone out and Estrellita has the key to their apartment, I will go and borrow his new hammer."

"We will wait," said Carlos. "When Mr. Fernandez returns, we will ask to borrow his hammer."

"Okay. We will wait," said Angel, looking at Carlos respectfully.

Format by Robin Sherwood
Set in Intertype Kenntonian
Composed by The Haddon Craftsmen, Inc.
Printed by The Murray Printing Company
Bound by The Haddon Craftsmen, Inc.
HARPER & ROW, PUBLISHERS, INCORPORATED